Dollhouse

by Mike Boyle

Thieves Jargon Press *** Somerville, MA

DOLLHOUSE

Thieves Jargon Press
PO Box 440051
Somerville, MA 02144

ISBN: 978-0-9770750-3-4

Printed in the United States of America

First edition, first printing: April, 2007

Cover photograph © 2007 by Robert Peyrebrune

Special thanks to Thieves Jargon Press, for believing in and offering editorial suggestions for this book. To my parents, who installed a love of books at a very young age. To Mary K, who gave me this wonderful old desk years ago. To any and all I've goofed with or traded songs, stories and poems with. To stepping out of life and putting it on the page and calling it life.

1   I woke up in Cindy's bed just before the sun came up and crept down the hall to the bathroom. Nick and Lonnie were angry because I had left and told them they'd have to take all the stuff back to our practice room. I gave them the $60 we made for the gig but they still whined about it. Cindy told me what all girls tell you, that I was better than them; they were dragging me down. I took a piss and washed my face in the sink, crept back.

Cindy lived with her mother in the suburbs. Her room was all lace and pastels. Yellow and rose canopy over the bed, pink and yellow pillows and stuffed animals littered around, dolls. A little girl's room. It didn't fit her. I had imagined black walls with posters, maybe black and red lights but it wasn't like that. I got back into bed and nudged her. Nothing; dead to the world asleep. I nudged her again.

"Oh, Cindy."

Nothing still. Good.

I got up and found her bottle of Dilaudid, took one and got my works and the spoon we had used the night before, crept back to the bathroom. I crushed the pill between the cardboard of a match pack and dumped it in the spoon, added water, and cooked it lightly. I laid out my arm, found my favorite vein and pulled at the plunger to check. Blood poured into the chamber. Good. I shot it and then waited a bit. Oh, yeah... I pulled the plunger back and did a boot. Mercy. I cleaned out my works and took them and the spoon back into Cindy's room.

I went downstairs and looked around. Nice. I turned on some lights and walked around for a while, looking for things I could steal. There was some good stuff. Paintings and knick-knacks. Fine furniture. I imagined myself cleaning the place out and having some fence give me a handful of money but I knew no fence and knew I was too lazy to even try it.

I turned on the TV and clicked at the remote. I had

never seen a remote control before, it was magic. I clicked through all the channels, nothing, it was early. Found the daily farm report and left it there. There was a pack of cigarettes next to the couch where I was sitting. I took one, lit it. The newscaster was talking about prices on the market. He talked about the drought in the mid-west. His hair looked greasy and was parted over a bald spot. I mused how I could do a better job than him. I could give the farm report life, nuance. But fuck the farm report. I stubbed out the cig, went into the kitchen and started looking around. I was hungry.

"Hey! Who are you?"

"Well, hello," I said. "My name's Tony."

She stood there in the doorway of the kitchen. She looked good. I smiled at her.

"Want some breakfast?" I asked her.

"Goddamnit!" she said.

"What?"

"Where's my daughter?"

"She's upstairs in her room."

She stomped off and I found a frying pan, some butter, some eggs and bread, and started making breakfast for all of us. No, I thought. I'm missing something. I rooted around in the fridge and found some sausage and orange juice. Then I found the coffee and made a pot while I worked on the rest. I heard some yelling upstairs and thought it was nice. She seemed nice.

She came back down.

"My daughter tells me you'll be staying with us for a while?"

"How do you like your eggs?" I asked her.

"What?"

"I'm making us breakfast. I'm a good cook. The coffee is done if you want some."

"Damnit to hell." She went to the coffee pot, grabbed a cup, and poured herself some. I opened the refrigerator and handed her the creamer and asked her, again, how she liked her eggs.

"Mmm, the coffee smells good. Can you just make a big omelet? That would be great."

"I can do that. Your name's Lois, right?"

"Yeah. I need a cig," she said and left the room. Good. The sausage was done and I took some paper towels and laid them on a plate. I drained off most of the sausage grease from the frying pan. Then I cut up some onion and green pepper and threw it in the remaining grease. I broke six eggs into a bowl and added milk and some spices, mixed it up and threw it in. I found some cheese and threw it on top and covered it while I made toast.

Then we were all seated around their fine dinner table in the dining room. Lois dug in and so did I. Cindy picked at it, ate little, then went back to bed.

"So, what do you do?" Lois asked.

"I'm a musician."

"Yeah? So what do you do?"

"What time is it?"

She looked over at the clock on the wall, looked back at me. I looked.

"Damn. I've got to get to work," I told her.

"Can you see that my daughter has dinner tonight? I'm meeting some friends after work."

"I'll take care of it."

I was about to run out the door and realized something, went to the phone and dialed. Some guy picked up.

"Hello?"

"This is Tony. Is Wendy there?"

"She doesn't want to talk to you."

"Look, be a guy for a slim second," I told him. "You can have her, I don't care. But be a guy, put her on the phone."

I heard a clunk and then silence. Then I heard, "Your

loser is on the phone."

She picked up the phone. "What?" she asked.

"Look, don't mess with my stuff, I'll come get it this weekend."

"Where are you?"

"I'm at Cindy's."

There was some silence. I heard her talking to the guy. What was his name? He was yelling something I couldn't quite hear. Greg, his name was Greg. Then the phone disconnected.

I dialed work and told them I was going to be late and then drove on over. All my clothes were out on the sidewalk. A light rain was falling. I scooped up my clothes and put them in the trunk of my car then I used my key, walked up. We had the top floor in the apartment building; the third floor. Greg met me at the top of the stairs. Wendy had him all pumped up and was continuing to say, "Don't let him hurt me. Oh, god, Greg, don't let him come in here!"

Greg was bigger than me and was wearing one of my shirts, some new wave thing Wendy had given me. I never liked that shirt.

"Look," he told me, "just go away and everything will be cool."

I looked up at him, told him nothing was cool. My stuff was out on the street.

My cat peered between his legs at me, Bruno. "Hey Brunoooo," I said. Greg kicked him and told me to go away again.

"You can have the woman but don't kick the cat."

"What you gonna do about it?"

I walked up and around him. He turned around and told me he was going to kick my ass. I looked at Wendy. She said, "Christ," turned around and walked into the bedroom.

"Go wait in the living room, Greg," I told him.

"Oh, man. You're just beggin' for it, ain't ya?" He cracked his neck and boxed his fists together.

"Do what he said, Greg honey," Wendy told him.

Greg honey stomped off into the living room. I petted my cat. He was glad to see me. "Brunooo," I said again. He purred and licked my hand.

A while later I was driving to work. There had been some negotiations. Wendy was keeping the cat and most of the furniture. I was coming back the next weekend to get my records, tapes and dresser. There had been some talk. Greg was really good in bed, better than me. He had a good job, better than mine. She was tired of playing second fiddle to my band and Greg wasn't a junkie. She had asked how Cindy was in bed and I told her I never kiss and tell.

"Oh, that's right. You're a gentleman."

"I try."

Truth was, we hadn't even fucked yet. We had just gotten high, talked and slept together.

"Let's not fight. Is Greg moving in?"

"We haven't talked about it."

"You'll be okay?"

"Yeah, I'll be fine. Thanks for asking."

She followed me downstairs when I left. "Please don't leave," she said. Nutty.

"I'm sorry but I have to."

She started crying. I hugged her, told her everything would be all right. I looked up over her shoulder and saw Greg honey looking down from the window. He pointed at me and held up his fists, banged them together again. I laughed. She pushed me away yelling obscenities.

2

I got to the plant an hour late. Vince the super was standing there as I walked up to my station.

"Where ya been, Diggs?"

"I had some things to take care of. Sorry."

"Well, I'm not mad. I'm whatcha call it? Cool. I'm cool about it. But your co-workers had to take up the slack. They might not be so cool about it."

I looked at the two other guys at the feeding station. They were sweating, lifting empty cases onto the line. Vince told me he wouldn't write me up this time and then said get the fuck to work, walked away.

Vince was old, must have been in his '40s. A real redneck. I had once seen him pull someone's tooth on the factory floor. The guy had been complaining about a toothache and Vince told him to go up to the bar on the corner at lunch, drink six shots of whiskey quick, then come back and 'ol Vince would take care of it. He did, too. Got some pliers on the guy's bad tooth and slammed him in the forehead. The guy fell back on his ass and Vince stood there with his tooth in the pliers and smiled. The guy spit blood, said, "Thanks boss," and Vince told him to get the fuck back to work.

I went up to the line and started heaving empty cases. Feeding the line was the worst job in the plant. Charlie looked over and asked if I had any weed.

"I'm all out. You guys been keeping pace?" I asked Ramon.

"It's been a bitch," he said. "Where the fuck you been?"

"Traded in the old lady for a new one but I fucked up. Didn't get my stuff from the old one's place yet. She threw it in the street."

The guys on the line would forgive almost anything for pussy stories. We ripped open skids and threw cases and I told them the story and added some fantastic lies. Ramon pulled out a joint, lit it. It was ridiculous, the things you could get away with at the bottling plant, so long as you did your job. The guys that ran the forklifts drank beer all day; had coolers on the back of their lifts. We worked by the dock doors and smoked weed constantly when we had it.

Then the buzzer sounded.

"Yeah!" Charlie said.

"Fuckin' A, yeah," Ramon said.

The buzzer only sounded when there was some problem up the line and they had to shut it down. We sat on a half-empty skid and finished the joint.

"So this Cindy's mom is hot too?"

"She's pretty hot. I think she likes me."

Some of the guys from capping came over and we bullshitted for a bit. Sometimes, during the lull of a dead line we had bottle fights. There would be broken glass everywhere. On occasion, the bottle fights erupted into fistfights.

I put an empty bottle on the floor and said I thought I could kick it up through the pipes close to the ceiling. They gathered around and I kicked it.

"Score!"

The bottle crashed to the floor somewhere in the rows of empty skids.

"Lemme try," Ramon said.

He set it and missed. The bottle went wide and crashed into the wall.

The others tried. Some made it but most failed. I did it again.

Charlie tried again and failed.

I did it again. Three for three.

The buzzer sounded and the line started up again.

That night I went back to Cindy's place, rang the doorbell and waited. Then I rang the doorbell again. And waited. Then I found some small rocks on the street and threw them at Cindy's window. She looked out and held up her finger. I waited. The door opened.

"Tony! You came back."

"What did you expect?"

"I thought… Well, never mind what I thought," she said and hugged me.

"You smell good."

"I took a shower. It's been a good day."

"I have some clothes out in my car that need to be washed."

"Get them. Bring them in."

I went out and got them. Armfuls of clothes. She showed me the laundry room and I dumped them on the floor. Then I went out and got the rest, telling her how Wendy threw them out in the rain.

I didn't know how to work the washer, Wendy had always done that stuff. Cindy showed me. Then we went upstairs and did some shots. She kissed me and told me I couldn't fuck her. That she had had an operation for the cancer. I didn't know. Cancer was something old people got. She told me it was ovarian cancer. That they had cut her up pretty good.

"You'll be okay eventually though, right?"

"That's what they say. They say they got it all."

I looked at her.

"I'll be able to fuck again, Tony. I'll just never have children."

"Okay."

"So, are you going to kiss me?"

We fell back on her bed. She told me to be careful, her belly still hurt. My dick got hard.

"I so want to fuck you," she said, feeling my cock through my pants.

"That's all right."

"Take off your clothes," she said. "I want to see your body."

"Take off yours."

"No, you."

I stripped, thinking I smelled from work.

"Mmm, you have a beautiful body. I'm gonna suck your cock."

"All right," I said.

She went at it.

"Don't come on my face. I want it in my mouth," she said.

She got it in her mouth.

Then I went and made us dinner. She didn't want to eat, I had to talk her into it. She tried and then felt better. I cleaned up after dinner. Did the dishes while she watched TV. She helped me with my laundry and we folded it on the floor in her room. Then we did some more shots. I asked her if she wanted to watch TV for a while and she said no, she just wanted to lay in bed. She stripped down to her underwear and t-shirt, crawled under the covers.

"You can."

"No. I'll stay here with you."

"You don't have to. Mom will be home soon. She'll probably be drunk."

"So what?" I asked as I stripped out of my pants and shirt, crawled under the covers with her. She leaned over and turned off the light.

"She likes you."

"She seems nice."

Cindy snuggled up against me and I lifted my arm, wrapped it around her.

"Was it hard today?" she asked.

"Work's always hard."

"Not work. With Wendy."

"It wasn't hard. I had to make sure she didn't throw anything else out on the street."

"You still love her, don't you?"

"No. That's done."

She didn't say anything, just snuggled against me. We

lay there breathing, looking at the ceiling.

"It was hard, wasn't it?"

"Yes," I told her.

She showed me her scar and I told her it wasn't bad, that she was still beautiful.

I awoke suddenly, heard someone downstairs. Living in the ghetto, I had chased burglars and thieves from windows and doors. They always ran and I always ran after them. Once, I had chased one in my underwear. It was winter. In the morning you could see my bare footprints in the snow following the shoe prints. They always got away and I always yelled they should never come back, that they should tell their friends I would kill them all. Eventually, the word got out on the street and nobody fucked with me or mine. Old habits die hard and I still slept lightly.

I sat up in bed and realized it was Lois. I got up, pulled on my pants and looked over at Cindy, who was sound asleep.

Downstairs, Lois was sitting on the couch with a drink in her hand and a cigarette in the other.

"Tony!" she said. "Come. Oh fuckin' hell, come sit and have a nightcap with me." She pet the empty couch beside her.

"What are you drinking?"

"Walker and water," she said, almost slurring her words. "Help yourself. You know where the bar is."

I wasn't much of a drinker but made myself a weak one, sat next to her.

"Want a smoke? Sure you do! Want my daughter? Aha-ha! You and every other scumbag."

She handed me a cig and lit it for me. I wasn't much of a smoker either, never bought them. She put her arm around my shoulder and started telling me about all the assholes she worked with.

"What do you do?" I asked her.

"What we do is run the county! Don't ever get a government job, you'll have to compromise. Oh, yes! You'll have to compromise 'til you forgot why you got into it. Haw-haw! Fuck them.

"And what do you do? Oh, yes, you told me you were a musician. Do you dance? Musicians should dance too, you know."

"I don't dance," I told her.

"Fine, fine, be punk rock. Fuck my daughter. Live in my house. I don't care."

"You care."

"Ha! You're funny man," she slapped me on the back. "Wait 'til you hit your forties. You'll be compromised by then. You'll be... what's the word?"

"Assimilated?"

"Ahh, man, you're smart. Yeah, that's the word."

She looked good. Still had her work clothes on; business suit, short dress, nylons, heels. She smelled good.

"I made dinner."

"Good, good. Did Cindy eat?"

"Yes."

She stood up and walked around the room for a bit talking this and that nonsense. She started making another drink and I got up, grabbed her around the waist and kissed her neck.

"No more drinks," I told her.

"Ohhh," she said. "That feels good."

She turned around and grabbed my hand, said, "Come on," and led me up to her room. It was much the same as Cindy's room, dolls and lace. I asked about the dolls and she told me they were family heirlooms, that her great-grandmother, grandmother and mother all made dolls. She walked me around and introduced me to them. They all had names. Then she babbled on about how her family came over on the Mayflower, that she was one of the

Daughters of the Mayflower.

I laughed. My grandfather came over on a death ship during the potato famine.

"Don't laugh," she said and pushed me back on the bed. "The daughters of the Mayflower are a very prestigious group. There's not many of us, you know."

"All right."

"Goddamnit, I want another drink," she said. "Could you go make me another drink while I freshen up? I have some candles in the hall closet. That would be romantic, yes?"

I went downstairs to make her a drink.

"So, do you make dolls?" I asked when I walked back into the room with her drink. She was in a black lace bra and panties, and was lighting the candles. She looked over her shoulder at me.

"Lois doesn't make dolls," she said.

3   Saturday came. Nick's buddy Jeff had a truck; they came over around noon and beeped the horn. I went out and we drove off to my old place, Wendy's place.

"How's it going there?" Nick asked.

"It's fine."

"Got any weed?"

"No, you?"

"Yeah, man. I got some, right Jeff?"

"Yeah, man, we got weed. We went down to that black bar on 3rd Street, Otto's? I know some guy that hangs there, a real nigger but he's always got weed. You ever been there? Freakin' niggers, junkies and whores, but I know this guy, right? We were in the insane asylum together down in Maryland a few years back. Yeah, the nut house. My parents put me in there cause I was a head, right?"

"Red light," I told him. He slammed on the brakes and I looked at Nick. He winked at me as he rolled up a joint.

"Yeah, anyway, my fucking parents put me in the nut house for being a head! Can you believe it?!"

"That's fucked up."

"Everybody's a head in the '70s! My friend's parents were cool about it, but not mine. You wouldn't believe the guys I knew, way bigger stoners than me, whose parents bought them cars and sent them off to college. But not mine! NO FUCKIN' WAY!" He started slamming his fists into the dash board.

"Green light," I said.

He stepped on the gas and we drove off. "Sorry. I got issues, man. Nick! Light that damn joint!"

Nick lit it, passed it to me and I took a hit, passed it to Jeff. He took a good one and held it. Then he blew out his hit and took another one. He spit a bit of weed from his lip on to the floor. He exhaled and handed it back to me. The end was all wet. We started across the bridge over the Susquehanna.

"Sheet pack," Jeff said.

"Oh, hell. Tony don't wanna hear this shit," Nick said.

"What? You don't wanna hear? I'm helpin' you, right? I'm helpin' you and you don't wanna hear?"

"No. Yeah. Sorry. It's been a hard week. Sure, I'd like to hear and thanks for the help."

"Yeah, well. Nick said you had some women problems. I know all about that. What's your name?"

"Tony."

"Yeah, shit. I know all about that, Tony. Who doesn't?" He drove on and we got to the red light at the other side of the river.

We got to Wendy's place and stopped.

"Oh yeah, sheet pack."

"Let's get this done first," Nick said.

Me and Nick left Jeff in the truck and went up to get my stuff. Wendy wasn't home, told me she couldn't bear being there when I moved out. Bruno was there – he met us at the top of the stairs. He was standing on a note from Wendy as well as a bunch of mail. I shooed him away and picked up the note and the mail, looked at the note for a bit. Words.

"Hey! We got playlists," I told Nick.

We had put out a single on our own label and sent copies out to radio stations. The playlists had been coming in the mail.

"Let's open them."

"No. Let's just get this done," I told him.

We got my dresser and records out to the truck after a few trips. I put my key on the table at the top of the stairs and said goodbye to Bruno. Nick had been asking me about Cindy, if she fucked as good as she looked.

"She's good in bed," I told him. Then he said I should

take my cat, but I said no. Wendy would take better care of him.

We drove over to our rehearsal room, where I was going to store my dresser and records. Jeff told me that a sheet pack is when they strip you naked, wrap you in wet sheets and shoot you in the ass with thorazine. Then he went on to tell me about pulling the lines off the air conditioner units to sniff the Freon in the nut house.

"Freon will get you high, man," he said.

4   I walked away from my job at the bottling plant. Charlie and Ramon probably thought I was going to the bathroom. Vince was standing by the door when I walked out and saw me but didn't say anything. I didn't even clock out.

It was good living in a place with no expenses, all I had to pay for was weed and gas money. I didn't even have insurance on my car. I just put in some random numbers at registration time. I walked out to the parking lot and got my bag of weed from the glove box and twisted up a joint. Then I drove out in the country for a bit, smoking. It was spring and the sun was shining. I rolled down my windows and smelled the good air. My '70 Mustang was paid for but the heater and radio didn't work. The odometer was rolling toward 200,000.

I pulled into the dollhouse's driveway a bit later. I took out my key, unlocked the door and walked in.

"Hey, honey, I'm home," I yelled and went into the kitchen, made myself a sandwich.

Cindy came bounding down the stairs. She had been getting better.

"What are you doing home so early?" she asked.

"I quit."

"No! What happened?"

"The supervisor came at me with a monkey wrench. Fucker's crazy."

"They can't do that! You have rights!"

"The workplace is not a democracy, Cindy. The plant manager was there urging him on. A crowd of people gathered around, mostly the suits. They were taking bets. I wasn't going to stoop to their level so I walked."

"That's fucked up. You need a shot."

"I thought we were gonna chill on the shots 'til the evening."

"Well, I need one."

She went back upstairs and got her kit, came back

down. I ate my sandwich, had a glass of milk while I watched her try to shoot up. She wasn't very good at it, had been trying to hit the veins in her wrist and hands lately. "Try your ankle," I told her. "There's a big vein there that nobody can see."

She put her leg across her other leg and looked at it, tapped the big vein there.

"Yeah, that one. I'll hold your leg."

She made the hit, blood poured into the fit and I let go. Then I finished my sandwich and milk, washed off the plate in the sink.

"Now you," she said, handing me the fit.

"I have a gig tonight," I told her. "Just weed for me today."

"Man, you're turning into a damn pot head."

"So?"

"My mom's got you drinking scotch with her too. That's disgusting."

"She's a refined woman," I told her.

"Man, this is getting weird. You're supposed to be my boyfriend."

"What?"

"Take a shot," she said.

"Could you make one for me?"

That made her happy. She crushed one up and put it in the spoon, cooked it lightly and sucked it up into the fit, handed it to me. I shot it and she said, "Yeah, man. We're going to hell!"

We were to go on at ten that night at Little Joe's, a dive bar on the eastern outskirts of Harrisburg.

It took Cindy a while to get dressed, a long while. I sat there while she tried on things and played with her makeup.

"Do you think Wendy will show up?" she asked.

"Who the hell cares?"

"You don't care?"

"It's a gig. People show up or not. We do what we do regardless of who's there."

I didn't want to get into it with her about our work ethic. The truth was, we were Nazis about our music. We played all-out every time. It didn't matter if we were just playing in our practice room or to a room full of people.

"I am so gonna look like your slut tonight," she said and did a model's walk around the room in what she finally decided on. She really was an awesome sight, short dark brown hair, big tits, beautiful ass all poured into a silk, low cut, black and pink polka-dot mini dress. She was gonna wear fishnets but I told her, no – wear the white nylons. The black four-inch pumps topped it off.

I sat there looking at her and a bit of hilarity gurgled up from my belly. It felt like insanity, like I might go laughing out into the street.

"Oh, god. You should see the look on your face. It works, doesn't it?"

I couldn't speak. A bit of drool pooled at my lip.

"Damn, Tony. You're such a geek. Does it work?"

I sucked the spit back into my mouth and told her it did.

"Do you need a shot?"

"A half might help."

We split a D and then walked downstairs. Lois was smoking, sipping scotch and watching TV.

"We're going, mom," Cindy said.

She looked over and said fine, go be punk rock, and turned her head back to the TV. Cindy stood there for a minute staring at her mom. I grabbed her arm and we went out the door to my car. I opened the door for Cindy and she sat. I closed the door and went around to my side, got in and started it. Cindy was crying.

"She wouldn't even look at us. We look great together

and she wouldn't even look."

"Don't worry about it," I told her.

"All right, I won't. But it hurts. Could you kiss me before we leave?"

We kissed. She wrapped her arms around me and held on, then let go, shook her head and said she was all right. We drove off.

"Do you love me?" she asked as I drove.

We got there around 9:30. Cindy started to open her door and I lay my hand on her arm, told her no. She giggled. I walked around and opened her door and she said, again, that I was such a geek. But she was delighted. I got my guitar out of the trunk and we went in.

The band we were to open for, Thee Fab, was already there, already had the PA system and all their stuff set up. I went over and said hello to Jim, their leader, and shook his hand.

"Who's this?" he asked.

"Cindy, Jim. Jim, Cindy."

He looked at me funny but didn't ask about Wendy. Guy stuff. Cindy said hello then walked over to the bar to get beer. He looked. The room was already a bit crowded. Everyone looked.

"Where'd you get that?"

"I have unbelievable luck."

"I'll bet she fucks like a beast."

"I'd like to think so," I told him.

Cindy leaned a bit on the bar and her dress hiked up. You could just see the edge of her pink panties.

"Goddamn," Jim said and looked away.

I saw Jim's wife at a booth across the room and wanted to wave but she was looking at Cindy also.

"Hey, Lonnie!" Jim said, just as he came in with his girlfriend, Monica. "We have everything set. You guys ready to play?"

"We're ready," Lonnie said.

Jim and I stood there talking this and that. Thee Fab had a big following and some fine equipment. We were going to use their stuff, drums, amps and all. More people started coming in, going to the bar and finding seats. I asked Jim about how they miked everything through the PA system and he explained how all the best bands did that.

"You guys never did that?"

"We just use the PA for vocals and maybe the kick drum with a snare ambient mike. We want our amps roaring, man." Translation: We had an old beat-up PA and couldn't afford that shit.

He explained that that wasn't the way to do it at all. That they played at low volume on stage and miked everything. Then the sound guy mixed it at the mixing board.

I walked over with him and the sound guy talked technical things at me.

"Got it?" Jim asked.

"Yeah, I got it."

I walked over to the booth where Lonnie, Monica and Cindy sat. I got out my guitar and tuned up. People came pouring in, it got crowded, really crowded. Nick came in at the last minute. We noticed the ace bandage on his arm and he told us about his train ride.

That night, he had to work late at the bakery. It was a big place, filled with ovens that made white bread for the east coast. He had no car or ride home so he hopped a freight train that ran over to where he lived in uptown Harrisburg. He hadn't figured the train would keep picking up speed, thought it would go slow through the city. He dove out at 7th and Division Street, got all skinned to hell, almost broke his neck.

"You're still bleeding, Nicky," Monica said.

"Yeah, fuck it," he said. Nick was a die-hard. He tuned up and we took the stage.

* * * * *

We started going through our set. It was horrible. The low stage volume idea sucked. The monster notes sounded like rain on a tin roof. After the first song I talked to the crowd.

"Does it sound all right out there?"

"Yeah!" some people yelled.

"Well, I'm glad it sounds good to you but it sounds like shit up here. Can you turn up the monitors?" I asked the sound guy. He shook his head and gave me the finger.

Some more people came in. Wendy came in with what's his name. The room was packed with people that, for the most part, I didn't know. Lonnie clicked his sticks to queue the next song and we went into it. We drove through our set, rapid-fire. There was much applause between songs. We drowned it out with the next ones. I stopped a few times to talk to the crowd. It was nice, I felt good about it but didn't stop long. Nick and Lonnie were a machine that needed to keep rolling. They looked at me like I was a dumbfuck, like I had forgotten how to be merciless. I played with them and the crowd, we played off each other.

We finished to applause and got off the stage. Jim went up and said, "Let's hear it for the New Left!" The crowd clapped some more and some people came up to us. There was talk. I always hated that part - it killed the illusion, made us mortal. Most bands lived for that, the fanfare; we didn't. It wasn't snobbery, it was just the way we were. We just wanted to play and leave. But the people were being nice. Some asked where they could get our record. I wasn't prepared for that – there was no place you could get it and I hadn't brought any.

Somebody said, "We just came to see you guys. Original music rules!"

Somebody else said, "We heard your songs on the radio."

Then, after a bit more talk and stuff, most of the people left.

A year earlier, we were doing what every other band in the area did, playing four forty-five-minute sets with fifteen minute breaks between. Most of the bands on the local circuit were cover bands, had no original music and were happy to play that stuff. We weren't; we had to fill up sets with obscure covers just to fill time. Then we decided, fuck that, and just worked on our own stuff. Nobody did that back then and it was fairly impossible to get gigs. The cover bands were pulling in the big bucks, but were kings of a small hill. We hated them all, pooled our money and put out a record. I sent them out in the mail to college radio stations. We got gigs at parties and punk shows. Eventually, we banded together with a few other bands and got gigs doing all original stuff sharing the bill in places like this. It had been a long climb. The cover bands still ruled the day but this small victory felt good.

Thee Fab took the stage as we went back to the booth where Monica and Cindy sat. Thee Fab wore costumes like the '60s bands used to wear, all matching. Stripes. They had some good original songs and sounded a bit like the Beatles, power pop stuff. The audience thinned out more, it was just us and their wives and girlfriends and a handful of others. I sipped beer and looked at them. Cindy said we kicked their asses tonight.

"Did it sound good?" I asked her.

"It sounded great."

I saw Nick up at the bar talking to some girl.

"You've got to quit stopping between songs," Lonnie said.

He was seated across the booth from me with Monica. Cindy rubbed her leg against mine. She pulled her foot out of her shoe and dug her toes on top of my white bucks.

"You wanna be the front man, Lon?"

"Fuck no."

"Then trust me, all right?"

Lon took a swallow of beer, looked at me and told me we had to kill them all, that we should never stop, that we should be relentless in our onslaught.

"They were with us tonight, Lon. And we still did what we came here to do."

Wendy came up and threw some mail on the table. She looked at Cindy and walked back to her booth with what's his name. She was all dolled up, but had a skinny man's ass. Cindy giggled. I looked at the pile on the table and opened things.

"Look Lonnie, more playlists!"

I tore them open and handed them around. Number 2 on the weekly charts at San Francisco State University; we had bounced Prince down the chart. Number 10 in Trenton, Number 6 at some college in Alaska, some others, France? I had sent something to France? I had forgotten all the places I sent the record to, but it was in the hundreds. I took care of all that stuff. Lined up the recording session, dealt with the people that pressed the records, got covers printed, cut and pasted them together, sent them out in the mail. There were some notes from DJ's also, asking when we were touring and such. I went over to thank Wendy for bringing it.

"You're welcome," she said. "How've you been?"

"All right. Things are a little funny. Everything okay with you and, uh…"

"Greg," Greg said.

"Yeah. Everything's fine," she said. "If you want, I'll keep your mail. It keeps coming in you know."

"That would be great."

"I'm still gonna kick your ass," Greg said.

Wendy looked at me. I looked at Greg. Then I walked

back to Cindy and sat down.

"Everything all right?" Cindy asked.

I told her everything was under control. Nick came over and said he was leaving with the girl he had been talking to. He grabbed his bass and left.

"Can you give me my share tomorrow?" Lonnie asked. "We're leaving too."

"Yeah, all right," I told him.

After they left Cindy asked me if it was always like that, if I always took care of everything.

"No," I lied. "They take care of a lot of stuff."

I went to the back room where the manager of the club was and he gave me our cut.

"You guys pulled in a big crowd tonight," he said. "I'd like to give you more but promised Thee Fab a certain amount."

He handed me $60. I thanked him.

"The crowd bailed after you guys left the stage. I want you back, soon."

"I'll be in touch," I told him and went back out. Thee Fab was still playing. There weren't many people there, just Thee Fab's wives and girlfriends and ten or so people at the bar. Wendy and Greg were drinking in their booth. Thee Fab went into a slow instrumental from The Ventures' *In Space* album. I took Cindy by the hand.

"We're leaving?" she asked.

"No. We're dancing."

We did a slow dance on the floor. She put her head on my shoulder and her arms around me. I put my right hand in the small of her back and took her other hand in mine.

"I feel wonderful," Cindy whispered in my ear.

"You are wonderful," I said and swung her out by the hand. She spun on her heels and smiled. I pulled her back. We were the only ones on the dance floor.

5

Cindy was all wound up and didn't want to go home. I asked her where she would like to go and she said, anywhere, everywhere. "I had such a wonderful time tonight. Did you see them looking at us?"

"They were looking at you, you look great."

"They were looking at you, too. I didn't know you knew how to dance."

"Neither did I."

"Oh, man. We were like Fred Astaire and Ginger Rogers. You got class, Tony. Real class."

I didn't know what to say. Nobody ever told me that before. Most of the time I just felt invisible.

"Let's just drive forever. Let's drive to California."

"All right," I said and drove on. We drove past the exit for her place.

"Here we go!" she said.

"Wheee! I said.

"Do you have any money?"

"I have eighty dollars and forty isn't mine."

"Damn. This isn't gonna work."

I pulled off the interstate and drove into Carlisle. There were some truck stops, no. There was an all-night diner. I pulled in. This time she waited. I got out and went over, opened her door. She placed her hand in mine and stood up. I shut the door and we walked in. There were some folks at the counter, looked like truckers and possibly some regulars. They looked bland, old. We found a booth in the corner and the waitress came over.

"Coffee," I told her.

"Two coffees?"

"And pie," Cindy said.

The waitress looked at me. "We have apple, cherry and lemon meringue."

I looked at Cindy. She said apple.

"Two apple pies then?" the waitress said to me.

"Yes, please," I told her and she waddled off.

"That bitch wouldn't even look at me."

"Forget it, Cindy. Small town stuff. They don't understand greatness."

"All right, I guess I am a bit dolled up."

"I recall you saying you wanted to look like my slut?"

"Ha! That's right. It still works?"

"Oh, yes – it works."

There was an old-time jukebox terminal at each of the booths. I started flipping through the tunes. Mostly country but I found some Sinatra, put in a quarter and picked two.

"One pick left Cindy. Pick one."

She flipped through and punched in *Secret Agent Man*.

"I was gonna pick that."

"I love Johnny Rivers. My mom has his albums."

"She's probably got Neil Diamond too."

"Oh, fuck yes. She's got all his stuff. Some of it was okay but I always liked Johnny Rivers way better."

Frank started singing. Some people from the counter looked over. An old woman nudged the man next to her and they both looked and smiled.

"*Solitary Man*."

"That's Neil's best song!"

"No doubt. Hey, check out the old couple." I head-gestured over to the counter. She turned around and looked. The woman was swaying her head to the music, then she put her head on the man's shoulder. She rubbed his back.

"You think we'll be like that?"

"I think we are like that."

She nodded and leaned across the table, kissed me. She grabbed my hands and squeezed them. The waitress came with the coffee and pie. We smiled at her.

"You folks don't look like no Frank Sinatra types but

I guess you can't tell from looking," she said. "Enjoy the pie. We have the best in town."

"Thank you ma'am," I said.

She put the bill on the table and said to pay at the counter when we were done. She started walking away and stopped, turned, leaned over and whispered something in Cindy's ear then pet her arm, walked away. Cindy smiled.

"What was that all about?" I asked her.

"Oh, nothing. Girl stuff."

"You aren't going to tell me?"

"I might. But not now."

We drank coffee and ate our pie while we listened. I looked out the window and saw nothing but my reflection. Then I looked at Cindy's reflection. She was looking off into space. Then she quickly turned her head and saw me in the window.

I took the long way back to her place, drove by the creek and showed her where I used to go fishing and swimming with my friends when I was growing up. I pointed out the diving rock and the tree swing that we used to swing out over the water on.

"Take me to the house you grew up in," she said.

"Let's not go there."

"Please?"

I told her okay and drove down the dead-end street I grew up on. The house was at the end of the street, by the woods.

"There it is," I said and started turning around to leave.

"No, don't leave. Can't we stop for a while? It's such a nice night."

"I'd rather not."

"Please?"

I pulled into the grass between the hedge and the woods; where I used to park when I still lived there. My parents' house was on the other side of the hedge. The lights were all out.

She got out. The sky was swollen shut. Nothing but stars and universe. The highway ran by on the other side of the woods. I got out and leaned on the hood of my car.

"Seen enough?" I asked her.

"Oh no, you must tell me," she said and walked around to me.

"There's the house I grew up in. There's the woods I played in. Seen enough?"

"Oh, no-no, you must tell more," she said and reached around me, pulled me off my car. "What do your parents do?"

"They're retired."

She grabbed me by the hand and pulled me into the yard. I remembered planting the trees there with my dad when I was a kid. I remembered the floods and the cookouts in the back yard. The garden was still there. My father was the greatest gardener in the neighborhood, possibly the country. He sweated and toiled at it. I helped.

"Who lives here, Tony?"

"My sister and parents."

"They're retired?"

"They're old, had me and my sister when they were old. I don't want to talk about it."

"You want me to tell you what the waitress said, right? God, what a beautiful night! No moon. I think all the stars are winking at us."

She let go of my hand and walked out into the yard. Don't. Don't let go Cindy. This is killing me.

"What was that song Thee Fab was playing? The one we danced to?"

"It was *Love Goddess Of Venus*; an old Ventures song."

"I love that song. It's running through my head."

Don't.

"Can we leave now?" I asked her.

"Okay, I'll tell you. That waitress said we made a fine looking couple and you were a keeper."

"That's all?"

"Yeah. I thought she was a bitch but she was nice. Everyone was so nice tonight."

"It's been a great night," I told her. "Now let's go."

I walked back to my car and started it. She walked back and got in.

"What's gotten into you? You were so nice and then you got mean. Are you going to tell me about it?"

I didn't say anything, just drove off. She looked at me and fidgeted, looked out the window, back at me.

"I haven't been down that street in years," I finally told her. "They kicked me out when I was twenty. I had nothing, nearly starved to death."

"That's horrible," she said and put her hand on my arm.

No. That's not horrible.

"Nick went through the same thing. That's why we're so tight."

"You guys are like family."

"Yes, we are," I said and drove on.

When we got back to the dollhouse the lights were out. We went up to her room.

"Families are hard," she said. "My parents divorced when I was eighteen. He still comes around to see me but it's not the same. It was like he abandoned us."

"What did he do?"

"He did the cliché thing; married his younger secretary. They have a big house up in Mountaindale. You know the place; really rich people live up there. Man, they even had kids. I have a stepsister and brother."

"He's rich?"

"He's that guy on TV, Tony. Bob Williams. I thought I told you."

She might have. I told her I didn't remember and took off my shirt. She stood there in the middle of the room looking lost. Then she kicked off her high heels.

"Tony?"

"Yes?"

"Would you dance with me?"

I would. We did the same dance we did earlier. Then she told me she was ready for me and stripped off her dress.

"Be gentle," she said.

I was.

6

Monday morning I drove over to the plant. My new time card was there. I clocked in and walked over to the line. Charlie and Ramon were already there, sitting on some empty cases and smoking. Waiting for the starting buzzer.

"Hey guys," I said.

"Where fuck you go Friday?" Ramon asked.

"Something came up."

"Got any weed?" Charlie asked.

"As a matter of fact, I do."

"Man," he said, "Vince is pissed at you for walking out. He came up later and asked us about it, said you didn't even clock out!"

"You think they'll pay me for the weekend?"

"No," they said in unison.

The buzzer sounded. It was seven. We worked four tens there, Monday through Thursday. The weekend crew worked three twelves. America ran on Coke.

We started tossing cases onto the line.

"Whatcha bring, Tony? Joints or a bowl?" Charlie asked.

When Charlie brought weed, he toyed with us, doled it out in one-hitters.

"Joints, Charlie."

"Fire one up, man!"

"No. Let's get the line fed a while first."

We heaved cases for half an hour. Then I ran to the front of the line and got some Cokes for us. Free Coke was the only perk of the job. We guzzled them down and went back to it. Ramon and I heaved. Charlie heaved but could never keep up with us. As usual, we had him slit the plastic off the skids that the forklift drivers kept bringing. We had him stack the skids we emptied. The pace was frantic. Ramon and I matched each other, case for case.

"Man. You guys gotta go balls out every day?" Charlie

asked as he opened another skid.

"We're getting a workout. Right, Tony?"

"Yeah. You oughta try it, Charlie," I said. "Work off that beer gut."

"It's not a beer gut, it's a Coke gut. Besides, I have a low metabolism."

"Yeah, right. You ever see the backseat of Charlie's car, Tony?"

"You mean his mom's car?"

Ramon laughed.

"Can I help it if my mom has a drinking problem?" Charlie asked and started heaving cases. "Ha, man, you fuckers are funny. Uh-oh Tony, here comes Vince."

I saw him coming. His hair was always one length – stubble.

"Diggs!" he yelled.

"Hey, Vince. What's going on?" I asked as I heaved cases.

"Step out, Diggs. We need to talk."

He walked away and I followed. He kept walking outside the plastic strips that hung over the back doors. He finally stopped outside.

"Where'd you go Friday?" he asked.

"Emergency in the family."

"What happened?"

"My dad is dying," I told him.

He blinked his eyes and then looked off. He turned around and looked at the hills behind the plant. When he turned back, his eyes looked a little wet. He handed me my paycheck and told me I should keep him informed. Then he walked out into the parking lot, turned and told me to get the fuck back to work. I put the check in my pocket and walked back in.

"You still got a job?" Ramon asked.

"Yeah."

We heaved cases 'til noon. The line did not stop once.

And neither did we.

At lunch break we smoked one of the joints in the parking lot. Nobody ate or had money for food. We sat in Charlie's car and he swilled down a couple beers, asking if we wanted any. No. Ramon and I just drank Cokes.

After work, I called my mother. I hadn't talked to her in months. She asked how I was and then said that she had been calling looking for me and Wendy told her I had moved out. That Wendy said she would call her when she got my new number. She hadn't heard from her so called back and some rude young man answered the phone.

"What did he say to you?"

"He was very rude, Anthony, I can't say it."

"Mom, what did he say? I want to know."

She told me he told her to stop calling there and called her a stupid bitch. I gave her my new number at the dollhouse.

"You aren't going to marry Wendy?"

"No."

"Good. She seemed like a real numbskull."

"I thought you liked her."

"I was just trying to be polite, dear son. Look, you should go visit your father."

"How is he?"

"He's the same. I don't care if you ever come here but you should go see him."

"I'm sorry I don't come around."

"No you're not. That's fine. Live your life. But go see him, Anthony."

She paused.

"What?"

"Don't go alone," she said.

Cindy and I did shots and then had dinner with Lois. We talked around things, just like a real family. I told them I had something I had to take care of and left, drove over to the hospital, parked and walked up, checked the nurse's station on the sixth floor and the nice lady pointed a finger down the brightly lit hall. I found the door, walked in.

There were tubes going out of and into him. There were wires and monitors. He was strapped down to the bed and shaking from the Parkinson's. Four months in a coma.

Half an hour later I walked back down the brightly lit hall and out to my car. He had almost come to, had stopped shaking and tried to talk, but it was too much of a reach. I told him it was okay and told him what I needed to tell him. He almost smiled.

I sat in my car, trying to breathe. Then I looked at my watch and drove over to Wendy's, parked across the street and lit a joint. Waited. A car pulled up across the street and I saw Greg get out. My timing was perfect. I took one last drag off the joint, stubbed it out in the ashtray and got out.

"Greg!" I called from across the street. Three lanes of cars whizzed by between us. He turned and saw me. I waved. He glared. I walked across the street when the light turned red down the block.

"What the hell're you doing here?" he asked.

I hit him square in the jaw and he staggered back a step.

"You fuck!"

He came at me, swung. I grabbed his wrist with my right hand, pulled it past me and kicked his legs out from under him, elbowed him in the nose when we landed, felt it pop inwards. He screamed like a girl and I got up, stood there.

"You gonna get up?" I asked.

He was yelling garbled nonsense.

"GET THE FUCK UP!"

He tried to grab my leg. I stomped on his hand.

Then I walked back to my car, re-lit the joint and took a big hit. I looked over at him. He was going to need a doctor. I exhaled and took another hit, started my car and drove back to the dollhouse.

7   The week went by. At work, it was much the
same: Ramon and I doing the bulk of the work and Charlie
opening skids, going to the bathroom, whining. Our idea
about having him open skids and take away the empties
had backfired because he had started acting superior,
like the opening and taking away of skids should be his
only job. On Wednesday, I started opening skids and told
Ramon he could have Thursday.

"Yeah. We'll trade off every day, right Charlie?"

Charlie agreed, but was a slow fuck. Ramon went off
about how he was doing all the work and told Charlie
he was going to kick his ass if he didn't pick up the pace.
Vince walked up to us to see what the problem was, saying they were complaining up the line.

"No gaps!" he yelled. "The cases need to be end to
end on the line or it doesn't work."

"Can't you slow down the line?" Charlie asked.

Vince just looked at him. "Why don't you just open
skids and take the empties away like you were doing?"
he asked.

"That's my job! It was their idea for us to trade,"
Charlie said.

Vince told us we shouldn't mess with a good thing,
that we should keep working like we had before, that we
were a good team. Then he walked away.

"We Charlie's niggers now," Ramon said.

"Looks like that. Hey, Charlie. You're gonna have to
do something. Us niggers ain't gonna be so frienly if'n
yous don't pitch in some."

Charlie didn't think it was funny. He worked slower
yet. We heaved the empty cases.

When quitting time came, Charlie ran off real quick
and drove away. Ramon and I walked out to the parking
lot and looked at each other. Then we got in our cars and
drove away too.

* * * * *

On Friday, my day off, Lois took Cindy to the hospital for tests in the early afternoon. She dropped her off and came back. We fucked and then she told me more about the dolls while I pretended to listen. My dad was in the same hospital, suspended in some wormhole. We went downstairs and she poured herself a scotch. I looked at the clock.

"Oh," she said. "Are you clocking me?"

"It's a little early, isn't it?"

"Don't ever forget who runs this house Tony," she said and drank it down. Then she poured herself another and asked if I wanted one.

"No thanks."

"Oh, that's right. You're on drugs with my daughter. Her drugs, I might add."

I didn't say anything.

"You think I didn't know? You think I don't smell the marijuana either? Huh?"

No. I didn't think she knew anything. It was actually rather uncomfortable.

"Should I make us some lunch?" I asked her.

She laughed and drank down her drink, set it on the coffee table and walked over to me.

"Relax, Tony. I'm not going to make you my slave but there are things you must do if you expect to live here rent free."

She wrapped her arms around me and kissed me. I grabbed her ass. She really did look good, an older version of Cindy, a marvelous fuck. But I had been having this ridiculous crisis of conscience ever since the night Cindy and I danced.

"I don't want to hurt Cindy," I told her.

"Nor do I. But there are things I want, fantasies, if you will, that I would like to live out. We will have to sneak so as not to hurt my daughter. I will continue to let you stay here rent-free and will also buy all the food. But there are things, yes?"

"What did you have in mind?" I asked while holding her there in the middle of the living room.

"For starters, practical things. You're gonna have to start doing the guy stuff around here. Cut the lawn, take out the trash and such."

Offering to help around the house hadn't even occurred to me. "That's fine," I told her.

"Good. The rest? You will see," she said. "Oh, this is going to be such great fun! I feel evil!"

For some reason she hadn't seemed real to me until then. I laughed and we fell onto the couch. Then she said she had to go pick Cindy up.

"Hold that thought," she told me.

A while later she came back with Cindy. I had eaten while I waited. A sandwich, some soup, a salad. Between the job, the band and the two women, I ate like a pig to keep up. I was still skinny.

"Whoo-hoo!" Cindy yelled when they came in the door. "I'm cancer free!"

She did a dance around the living room floor and I went to her, hugged her.

"Mom! Tony's a great dancer! You should have seen us the other night at Little Joe's! He was fabulous!"

I twirled her around the room. She laughed and I dipped her, kissed her neck, then we twirled some more. Lois clapped and said it was marvelous. She looked happy and ran over to her stereo, turned it on and put on a record. Bobby Rydell. Then she poured herself another drink and watched us.

Bobby Rydell sang *Volare*. We were in magic land.

"Mom! Could you put on some Neil Diamond?" Cindy asked.

"You don't like this?" Lois asked, and added that she was a huge Bobby Rydell fan from way back.

"It sucks," Cindy said. "Neil rocks, right Tony?"

"Uh..."

"You damn punks," Lois said and went digging. Cindy and I stood there, looking at each other. Her eyes were shining. Lois found Neil's *Hot August Night*. Goofy.

We danced slow around the room. Cindy put her head on my shoulder. Lois said she was going to make dinner for us and went into the kitchen with her drink and her smokes.

After dinner, Cindy walked up to her room and I looked down at Lois. She looked sad but winked at me. I followed Cindy up. We stripped down to our underwear and she put a record on her stereo, The Psychedelic Furs. She broke out the pills and we did shots. I rolled a joint and we shared it in bed. Then she started playing her other records. Some of it I hadn't heard before. She played DJ and I lay back.

"This is cool, right?" she asked.

"Hell, I don't know."

"What do you mean you don't know? My friend Stacy says this is the cool stuff. I don't understand it but I trust her judgment."

"You what?"

"She's a club girl and keeps up on things. I trust her."

"That's asinine," I told her. "Either you like it or you don't."

"What the fuck, you know? INXS is hot, man! You guys don't even play the big clubs in town."

"Could you just turn that shit off? The Furs are cool, but this sucks," I told her.

She said she had another Psychedelic Furs album and put it on. Then she got into bed with me.

"You fuck better than you dance," she said.

"I don't know anything about either".

"Should I show you?"

"Yes," I told her.

The record rolled on and the needle lifted. I leaned over and turned off the light.

8   That weekend we had a party at our rehearsal room. I met Nick and Jeff at the room around six. Jeff brought a tub and tap; I brought the keg and ice. Nobody thought of cups. I told them I'd go get them, I had to go back to get Cindy anyway.

Since it wasn't an actual event, just a party, Cindy didn't get dolled up. Lois had. She was going to meet friends at a fashionable restaurant/bar and walked out with us saying how fantastic it all was, that we should have a grand time and she would do the same with her friends. She hugged Cindy and told her she loved her then drove off in her BMW. Cindy jumped up and down and clapped as her mother drove off. She was beaming, a beautiful light.

When we got back, Lonnie and Monica had arrived. It was still early; the party wasn't supposed to start 'til eight. As usual, we didn't advertise, had just made a few phone calls. There was to be a charge at the door, two bucks a head, just to cover the beer expense. We had invited another local band over to play but they hadn't arrived yet.

"Hey kids," I yelled as we walked in. They said hi and I handed out plastic cups. We all tapped beers then sat on our couch and on the old chairs. Nick lit a joint and we passed it around. Lonnie didn't smoke weed and Monica said she shouldn't but took a hit, passed it to Jeff.

"Weed makes me crazy," Monica said.

I sat on the arm of the chair Cindy was sitting in and she had her arm around my waist. We had been cutting back on the shots, were down to one D each a day. Cindy jumped up and said, "I want to look at your stuff!" and walked over to our amps, drums and such. Monica did the same. Then they stood in the corner talking girl talk.

* * * * *

I flashed back to a few months ago, when I was still with Wendy. We had gone to Lonnie's place, the basement in his mother's house that had been converted into an apartment. It was up in the mountains to the southwest of Harrisburg. I went to use the phone and noticed a picture of a cunt in the middle of the dial. I dialed and the cunt whirled around. Of course, I knew whose cunt it was, it was Monica's. I knew Lonnie was a camera freak and dug taking pictures of his women. I also knew Monica was an exhibitionist. I got done with my call and hung up, went back to drinking.

I saw Monica looking at me while I droned drunken talk with Lonnie. A bit later, I went up to my car to get another pack of smokes and when I came back in, Monica met me in the upstairs hall.

"How'd you like the picture on the phone dial, Tony?"

"You're a freak," I told her.

"What do you think of these?" she asked as she lifted her shirt to show me her tits.

"You have nice tits, Monica. Now let's go back downstairs and get more drunk."

I tried to walk past her and she blocked me, holding her shirt up like that. She was drunk. I was working on getting drunk but booze never really loosened me up like that.

She licked her finger and made little circles around her nipple.

"Look at my titties, Tony. Don't you want to suck them?"

I grabbed her arms and pulled her shirt down, told her Lonnie was my friend. We went back downstairs. Lonnie gave us a curious look as Wendy babbled nonsense. Later on that night I said I was thinking of putting a hood ornament on my car. One of those casts they do for rock stars, of my cock. I was a funny guy.

"You're gonna put a limp dick on the hood of your car?" Monica asked.

We all laughed. Wendy laughed longest.

Marla, Monica's sister, showed up all wild-eyed. I was going to ask her for two bucks, but it was still early. Besides, she was a friend from way back. I said hello and got up, poured her a beer.

"Hey guys. Where's Monica?"

"Hi Marla," Monica yelled from the other side of the room. "What's going on?"

"I, ah… Well, things are fucked up," Marla said.

"Where's Doug?" I asked.

"Man, Doug went off somewhere. Philadelphia or something. Man! This place is a mess! I brought a broom and dustpan. It's out in my car."

She went out to her car and brought her broom and dustpan back in and went at it. We lifted our feet and then got tired of that, went to the other side of the room. Marla was a speed freak.

"I don't see how you guys can live like this!" she said.

It was true, the floor was crunchy. There was broken glass everywhere. We would fling empty bottles toward the closet in the far corner when we were playing but rarely made it. We had finally resigned ourselves to just smashing the bottles on the floor.

She was a hurricane, really went at it. "Got a trash can?" she asked.

"No. Just throw it in that closet in the corner," Nick said.

She looked in the closet and almost went insane. "What the hell is this? Broken bottles and 2x4s?"

"It's the trash can," I told her.

"Do I have to bring you guys a proper trash can?"

"Yeah, probably. Nick? Give that woman a joint," I

said.

He gave it to her and lit it for her. She took a big drag and handed it back to Nick, then went to sweeping all the debris into the closet. Then we all sat down.

"Thanks, Marla," I said. "It really looks nice in here now."

"I can't believe you guys," she repeated.

Nick handed the joint back to her. "Smoke the whole thing," he said.

She finished her beer and I got her another.

Blacklisted showed up with their gear and girlfriends. They were to play the first set. They set their stuff up, got beers. It was 7:30. Showtime was eight. We barely had time to chat before people started showing up. Monica took the money at the door and pointed them to the keg. Nick, Lonnie and I drank and smoked, talked. More people showed up. I didn't know how it worked, had just made a few phone calls and then all these people. People we knew and many we didn't. By the time Blacklisted took the stage it was really crowded. Monica gave me a handful of money and I counted it. We had paid for the keg and more.

More people came in. Blacklisted played for an hour. Then some people started yelling, "New Left!" Nick, Lonnie and I waited for Blacklisted to clear off their stuff and I went up to the microphone. People clapped and yelled.

"We're coming on in a bit," I told them and walked back to Cindy, asked her if she was all right.

"It's a crazy night," she said. "Who are all these people?"

"I don't know. Let's walk outside for a bit."

We walked outside and looked at the stars. There was a crescent moon.

"What are you doing, Tony?"

"What?"

"Your people are in there."

"I don't know them. I know you. We're walking under the stars."

The parking lot was full. I heard some people walking up from the street. They rounded the corner of the building to the back. It was Wendy, her brother and a couple of her girlfriends.

"Hey, Diggs!" Wendy said. "I hope it's okay we came."

I told her it was fine and said hello to them. Cindy grabbed my arm like, my man now, and coolly said hello.

"We're just about to play," I told them. "Let's go in."

Monica charged them at the door.

"Where's what's his name?" Cindy asked Wendy.

"Greg? He hasn't been feeling well," she said. "Right, Tony?"

We started our set with *SBD (Silent but Deadly)*. During *Ten Car Pileup*, the crowd was yelling the chorus back at us. "We were first in line!" they shouted.

The beer ran out and someone went to get a few cases. They handed us beers and we played on for a hour or so, going off our set list and doing some old cover tunes we used to play. Phil, from Blacklisted, came up to jam with us and I handed him my guitar, sang *Down on the Street*, the Stooges tune. We went through a couple other Iggy songs as well. *Dirt* and *TV Eye*. Phil handed me my guitar back and sang *Happenings Ten Years Time Ago*, the old Yardbirds song. We tore it up and ended there.

Then, people were leaving and milling about in some dazed state. Some guy came up to me and said he would like to manage us, told me his name and said we could have made great money charging a dollar a beer at our parties.

"It's not about that," I told him.

"Look. I put on these shows and want you guys to play at them," he said.

"What's your name?"

"Mick Angst. I do these hardcore shows, see? Have bands from all over the country."

"So you say. Is there any beer left?"

There was no beer left. I said thanks to Blacklisted as they walked out. I guess Marla had gone to get trash bags because she was cleaning up.

"Marla!" I yelled. "You don't have to do that. Leave the bag. I'll get it tomorrow."

"I'll get it tonight, Tony."

"Marla! Goddamnit. Just stop. Relax. You've done enough."

She stopped and looked at me.

"I don't know what to do with myself!"

"All right, Marla. Carry on."

She smiled and went back to it. I heard some yelling outside and went to look. It was Monica. She was freaking out, yelling at the top of her lungs. She ran over to the bank next door and tried to break its windows with rocks she picked up in the parking lot. Then she just slammed her fists against the glass, saying the cops would come and she would fuck them up. Lonnie just stood there. Nick, Cindy and I went to her, dragged her off the building. She pushed us away and started taking off her clothes, winging them this way and that.

"You want a picture of this, Lon?" she yelled.

Lonnie continued standing there, frozen.

We picked up her clothes and, after some struggle, got her in Lonnie's car. They drove off.

I kicked the rest of the people out and locked the door. Mick Angst had given me his number. I threw it in the parking lot.

9

I was halfway through cutting the back lawn when Lois walked up to me. I shut off the lawnmower. She handed me a lemonade. I drank it down and handed back the empty glass.

"Analingus," she said. "Think about it."

She walked back into the house. I looked at her ass then started the lawnmower and went back to it.

Two hours later, I was done with the lawn and the hedges and was soaked with sweat. I went inside. They had central air conditioning, another thing I never knew of. Lois and Cindy were watching TV together in the living room.

"The lawn and hedges are done," I said, walking into the room. They didn't say anything, were watching some movie. "You're welcome. I'm going to take a shower."

"Thanks, Tony. Go take a shower," Cindy said.

"Thanks, Tony," Lois said.

It was June and summer was bearing down. Cindy was all better now. We had done the last of her Dilaudid a month ago after tapering off and hadn't suffered too much. Cindy wanted me to get us some stuff but I told her no and held my ground. She eventually relented. Just last week she had said it was good we had cleaned up, she felt good. We still smoked weed but that was nothing. Lois was another story.

I took a shower and changed, then smoked a couple hits in Cindy's bedroom. It was Saturday afternoon and I was bored. There was nothing much to do. I called up Lonnie and asked him what he was doing. He said him and Monica were thinking about going out to see Thee Fab.

"You wanna come?"

"Man, I dunno," I told him. "I called the booking agent at the Metro again this week, did I tell you?"

"Why even bother?"

"Fuck. I dunno."

"What did he say?"

The Metro was the biggest club in the area and the booking agent there also managed bands. His boys played cover songs to the cokeheads and the fashionable crowd that frequented the big local clubs. When they mixed in some of their own songs, they were MTV-Lite. There was no interest in anything different, even if it was great. "You guys have no draw, no image, just play weird violent shit," is what he told me.

"Let's go over there some night and fuck him up," Lonnie said.

"Ahh, hell. The hell with him. The hell with this town. Man, I'm bored. Let's just get together tonight and play."

Our regular practice schedule was Tuesday, Thursday and Friday nights, leaving the weekends open for fun.

"I'm up for it. Call Nick and call me back."

I hung up, dialed Nick. He had quit his job at the bakery and was working as a cook in some hotel downtown. He had moved out of the rooming house and in with some guy named Don, who had an apartment uptown and was the chef at the hotel.

When Nick picked up the phone, I told him the plan and he said he was up for it but I'd have to come get him.

"I'll be over at seven," I told him and hung up, called Lonnie back and told him 7:30.

When I walked downstairs, Cindy was lying on the couch and clicking through the channels with the remote.

"Scoot," I told her and she picked her feet up so I could sit.

"We going out to the Metro tonight?" she asked. She had been bugging me about it, how we should be seen!

"No," I told her. "I'm going to practice. You can come if you like."

She kicked at me and said she talked to Stacy, that Stacy was going to the Metro like she did every Saturday night and she might just go with her. "The Revenge are playing tonight," she told me. "Don't you want to see them?"

The Revenge was one of the bands the guy who ran the Metro managed, his biggest band. I imagined all the halfwits across the country blindly following bands like them. They were the enemy.

"No."

"We need to go out dancing, Tony. I want you to take me out dancing."

"I can't do it," I told her. "I hate them."

"Man! You don't know how to have fun," she said and got up, stomped upstairs.

I turned off the TV and went into the kitchen where Lois was. She was making dinner and drinking. She was already a bit looped.

"What're you making, Lois?"

"Some freakin' lasagna and a salad. It's gonna be good. Be a dear, go make me another drink and get my pack of smokes from the living room?"

She handed me her glass and told me to just fill it with scotch. I went out and got her drink, made myself a light one, went to the faucet and added water. Then I got some ice cubes from the freezer and added them to my drink.

"Two cubes for me," Lois said.

I put them in and gave it to her. She put the lasagna in the oven, turned around and told me to let Cindy go out with Stacy, have some fun. Then she leaned under the sink and pulled out this contraption, showed it to me.

"What's that?" I asked.

"It's an enema, dear."

She swilled down half her drink and took my hand. I followed her into the downstairs bathroom. She filled

the bag up with warm water and handed me the hose.
I stood there.

"Oh, my. You should see the look on your face!" she
said. "Relax. I'll show you what to do."

She got some petroleum jelly out of the cabinet and
lifted up her robe. Then she bent over, rubbed a finger
full of lube into her ass and told me to insert the hose.

"You've done this before?"

"No. I have books about it. Now put the hose up my
ass, please."

I did. She squealed lightly and then told me to squeeze
the bag of water into her ass.

"Ahh," she said. "Get it all in there."

"It's empty," I told her.

She stood up and pulled her robe off, threw it on the
floor. Then she bent over the bathtub and asked me to tap
her asshole with my finger. "Tap it like a drum."

I did. She moaned a bit and my dick started getting
hard.

"I'm gonna fuck you," I told her.

"No, don't! I'm going to shit!"

I backed away and she went down on the toilet and
let it fly. I put my cock in her mouth and she sucked on it.
The bathroom smelled of her shit. She got up and flushed,
wrapped her arms around me and kissed me.

"Let's go upstairs now," she said, taking my hand.

"What about Cindy?"

"Her tantrums last at least a half-hour. Don't worry
about it. She'll be in her room with the door locked and
probably playing her stereo loud."

Lois was right; we could hear the stereo thumping
from down there.

Nick and I tuned up our guitars then sat on the couch,
smoking weed. He was singing and playing my guitar,
showing me a new song he wrote. It was a little rough,

there was something there but I knew I would have to make up another guitar part. I had a new one also. He handed me my guitar and I sang it for him. Lonnie came in while I was playing the thing.

He set the case he brought on the floor and ripped it open, handed us beers. We dicked around with the new songs for an hour or so, trying this and that arrangements. You can only do so much in one night, we knew they weren't right yet but knew if we let it jell a bit that we'd have them worked out by next week.

We took a break and sat on the couch, smoking and drinking. Someone knocked on the door. I went over and opened it. It was Mick Angst with a few people.

"I thought you guys would be here," he said. He had brought beer also and introduced us to his friends. We all sat around and drank for a while. Then we roared through a set, since we had a bit of an audience. Angst had been coming around and we had played at a few of his all-age punk shows by then. He tried to set us up with a few gigs in Pittsburgh and Philadelphia but they were showcases for no money and I had turned him down. "You guys need to do these shows," he insisted at the time. "They're playing your records and people know you there."

"A real manager would get us some money," I said, but he insisted we had to showcase. I tried to tell him that once you're their bitch you'll always be their bitch, and he just looked at me.

After kicking Angst and his friends out, we went over to the Metro. I knew the doorman from the old junkie days and he let us in for free. The Revenge was playing. Fuckers. I wondered what Beethoven would have done with a machine gun. We went to the bar and got beers. The barmaid just gave them to us.

"I fucked that girl in a graveyard," Nick told us, laughing, after we asked about the drinks.

Some people came to our table and pulled up chairs. I

saw Cindy sitting with Stacy and a few guys at the other end of the room. She hadn't seen us. I knew one of the guys, a real coke hound who dealt on the side. He was a liar and a cheat, had once sold me something he said was dope that was actually angel dust. He even watched me shoot it, then laughed when I went crazy for a while. I told him I was gonna kick his ass and he laughed some more because I couldn't get up off the floor. It was no damn wonder my parents had kicked me out.

I drank down my beer and walked over.

"Hey, Cindy!" I said.

"Hey! What are you doing here?"

"We all came out after practice. Hiya, Stacy. Hello, Dwayne."

They said hi and Dwayne gave me a look. "I was just telling Cindy how we went way back, right, Cindy?"

"You didn't tell me that," she said.

"Did he tell you he has coke?"

"Yeah. But all the guys here say that."

"Dwayne probably has some really good coke for himself. Then there's the shit he sells. Right, Dwayne?"

"You can't just slander a man like that Tony. I have something good. Let's go into the bathroom and I'll turn you on, man. Shit. Look at you. We go way back, right?"

I pushed my open hand into his face and he fell back on the floor in his chair. His two friends jumped up and started at me. I just looked at them. They stopped, then picked Dwayne up off the floor. Dwayne dusted his bad self off and told them to leave me alone, laughed.

"I have connections and know people, but I'm gonna let that slide."

"Cindy? Would you come with me?" I asked her as I put out my hand. She took my hand and got up. Stacy got up to go with us.

"You were lucky tonight, Tony!" Dwayne yelled at

me.

I ignored him, walked Cindy over to our table. "You like those freaks?" I asked her.

"They're just guys," she said. "Just guys being guys. Stacy and I were bored so we let them sit with us and buy us drinks."

"They're creeps."

"I'm glad you showed up. This is nice."

They sat down and I said I'd be back and walked back over to Dwayne's table. The Revenge was playing Clash songs, poorly. The dance floor was filled. Dwayne saw me coming and said something to his friends.

I still remembered Dwayne as the snot-nosed kid who would try to tag along with us older kids back in the burbs. We had treated him badly but eventually let him hang after hearing horror stories about his home life. I sat down and asked him how his brother was. His older brother was a local football legend, could have gone to any college in the country but got drafted right after high school. Went to Vietnam.

Dwayne told the other guys to leave the table, that we were going to talk.

"He's still in the VA hospital in Allentown," he told me after his friends left. "I went to visit him last month. Man, he's still all fucked up."

"How long's he been in there now?"

"Ten years."

We talked for a while and I asked him where he got the muscle.

"I'm involved with some high-level dealers now. Met the Colombians and everything. You wouldn't believe it. You sure you don't want some lines? I'll lay a few on you."

"Nah, coke ain't my thing. I'm too wired as it is."

"You still fucking with dope?"

"I cleaned up."

"That's good."

"Yup. Look, you take it easy, all right?" I said as I got up to leave.

"We even now?"

"No," I told him. He pointed at me and winked.

Stacy bought us a round of drinks; beers and shots. I danced with Cindy. I did knee dives and the backspin. I did dances nobody ever heard of, took a running start and skidded across the dance floor on my back while I mused about those huge steel structures that carried the high voltage wires from Three Mile Island, how they looked like something out of *War of the Worlds*, that it might be cool to scrape the landscape like that.

The Revenge finished their set and came to drink with us at our table. Tons of people gathered around, we pulled a bunch of tables together. Cindy was happy, it was an event. The guitarist of The Revenge leaned over and told me, "Look, man. I have these words."

"What?"

"I have these words for a song, man. You want to write the music to it?"

"Why don't you get one of your guys to do it?"

"It's about this chick that fucks the devil," he said, like that explained everything.

I looked at the sheet of paper, his handwriting was barely legible. He pet me on the arm and said, "Call me when you're done."

"Right," I told him and put the words in my pocket. Devil words in my pocket and Nick fucking some barmaid in a graveyard and huge steel structures scraping the landscape. As long as the girls smile that long smile.

They kicked us out at 2:30. Everyone drove off. We found the club manager's car and pissed all over it.

10

It was late Sunday morning when I woke up. Light was pouring in the window, it hurt. I got up to close the shades and the sheet was stuck to my back. When I sat up it pulled off like a band-aid. I closed the shades and looked at the clock. Almost eleven. Stacy and Cindy were still asleep and the bed was a mess. The images that rolled through my head were more a meat painting than a movie. I pulled on my leather pants and went to the bathroom to piss. I went downstairs to make coffee and noticed Lois, sleeping on the couch with an empty bottle next to her. I made coffee and started making home fries. In another frying pan, I threw in some sausage patties. Meat slide shows, flicking by – freakin' tequila. I remembered having a piss distance contest with Nick and Lonnie. Everyone's good at something, but is it marketable?

"God, Tony. Please make me a drink. I have a terrible hangover," Lois said behind me. She looked like hell but I didn't say it.

"No, Lois. You gotta eat. I'll make us something good. Have some coffee."

"Oh, god. Food." She ran into the bathroom. I could hear her, it sounded bad.

I poured V8 into a juice glass, went to the bar in the living room and opened her last bottle of scotch, poured her a small one, then knocked on the bathroom door.

"Don't come in here!"

I opened the door. She was lying on the floor.

"Drink the scotch, then drink all the juice," I told her.

She did and handed me back the glasses.

"It's gonna stay down?"

She breathed in and nodded.

"Take a shower," I told her. "Then you gotta eat, all right?"

"I'll try."

Burn, Lois.

I went back to cooking and when it was done I took coffee up to the girls. Burn, girls, burn. We're going to hell. They woke up and I gave them steaming cups. They were hung over, kicked me out of the room saying they were going to shower.

"Hurry the hell up," I told them. "I have breakfast waiting."

"He's our houseboy," I heard Cindy say to Stacy as I shut the door.

I wasn't hung over, just hungry. I made toast and piled a plate full of eggs, home fries and sausage and wolfed it down. Lois was back on the couch, groaning a bit. I looked in the medicine cabinet in the hall and found some Alka-Seltzer. I put two in some water and poured her another juice, took it to her.

"What's gotten into you, Lois?"

"Ahh, hell, Tony. Save it."

"All right. I'm gonna make you some toast."

"Stop. Just stop it. I'll get something for myself later. Thanks, but stop."

After breakfast and a shower, I drove Stacy home. She had left her car at the Metro, said her friend downstairs would give her a ride to get it later. We went past my old place and I saw Greg's car out front.

"That's where I used to live," I told her as we went past.

"Oh," she said, and gave me directions to her place further uptown. Stacy was five foot nothing with small tits but a marvelous ass and a cute face. She had short hair. I liked girls with short hair, thought they were possibly more practical than girls with long hair. Wendy had very long hair. I would sometimes be at work or someplace else and feel something funny, go to the bathroom and pull one of her long hairs out of my underwear.

"Here we are," she said.

I stopped in the street.

"Nah, park. Come up. You want to come up?"

"Sure," I told her. "Why not?"

I found a spot and we got out.

"That's a '70 Mustang, right?"

"Yeah."

"The last good year for them was '69. They started putting emission controls on them in '70."

"I tore all that shit out of it after I bought it," I told her. "It pushes around 220 horsepower."

"No shit. You a motorhead?"

"Used to be."

"My brother's a motorhead. He's got a '69 GTO."

"Gas, tires and oil," I said.

"Oh yeah, man. You know. I grew up around all that stuff. My dad has all kinds of cars. He's got a '67 Shelby Cobra. His pride and joy."

"That's the coolest car ever!" I told her.

"No doubt. Man, your car looks like shit though. Come on."

I followed her ass up to the apartment, explaining the hard decision I had to make, that I couldn't afford keeping my car up in style and still play music. That I had to pay for a rehearsal room, instruments and strings, that I still talked to some of the old motorheads I used to hang with.

"Poor baby," she said. "Cindy said you could be a geeky motherfucker."

"Oh, shit. Have I been babbling?"

"Ahh, forget it. It's cool. Let me give you the tour."

She showed me around and told me she was a legal assistant, did research for some lawyers. That it paid good. It was a big one bedroom place on the top floor of an old building. The tour ended on her big balcony overlooking a yard filled with trees. She had several houseplants out there, hanging from holders.

I told her it was nice. "Like a tree fort out here."

"I love. Would you like a drink? I have beer."

"No beer," I told her, and sat down on one of her rattan chairs. She sat on a chair on the other side of her little table.

"Good," she said. "My ex boyfriend used to drink beer all day."

I didn't say anything.

"The birds come up here to my feeder. Sometimes I sit here real quietly and watch them."

"Birds, trees. coffee. I could dig some coffee."

She said she'd go get it and I looked out over the garden. It was pretty. There was something I should have been doing. No, there's nothing you can do, really. A bit later she brought out coffee for us, apologizing that it was instant.

We smoked a bowl looking out over her yard, not saying much. We drank coffee. Some birds few up to her feeder and she reached over, grabbed my arm and held her finger over her lips. "House Finches," she whispered. We looked at them 'til they flew off.

"I'm not gay," she then said.

"What?"

"What we did last night. I'm really not a lesbian. Please don't tell anyone. I know guys like to brag about shit."

"I won't tell," I told her.

"Look at me and tell me, Tony."

I did and she seemed satisfied.

"Want some codeine?" she asked. "I've got 4's."

"I'd better not. Been trying to stay away from opiates."

"Yeah, that's what Cindy said. She said you've been a real trooper, helping her out and stuff. We did some last night. She did two."

"It's no good," I told her. "I have to get back."

I stood up to leave and she told me that I could come over anytime, that nobody had to know. She gave me her phone number; I put it in my wallet and turned to leave.

"Wait," she said and walked off.

Then she was handing me four Tylenol #4's.

"You can give them to Cindy or keep them for yourself, all right?"

"All right, Stacy."

"May the 4's be with you," she said, and kissed me.

"Funny." I put them in my pocket. "See ya around."

"Call me?"

"Right."

When I got outside, I threw them in the street, got in my car and started it. Then I got out of my car and picked the pills up, put them back in my pocket.

11

I was given a three-day paid leave of absence for a death in the immediate family. The funeral wasn't until Wednesday. I worked Monday and Tuesday. Horace, the plant manager, walked up to me Tuesday afternoon and gave me a basket full of fruit with a card and said he was sorry. I looked at it. Vince was standing there.

"That was nice of him," I told Vince after he walked away.

"He's an idiot," Vince said. "I'm sorry too, kid."

Charlie and Ramon chimed in their sorries as well, and we went back to heaving cases.

Wendy showed up at the funeral and found me, sitting a few rows behind my family. She said she was sorry and we talked in the parking lot afterwards. She said she missed me, sometimes, and didn't mention me beating up her boyfriend.

On Friday, I drove upstate, where my mother and father came from, for the burial service in St. James Cemetery. It was just a half mile from the Pennsylvania border and I saw many relatives I hadn't seen in years. Everyone was sorry. Sorry was just a word people used when there were no words.

Sometime during the burial service I wandered out into the graveyard to find my father's parents' headstones. I wasn't missed; my mother had taken my brother-in-law's hand and had him sit next to her for the service, leaving me standing there. An older woman walked up to me.

"You're him, aren't you?" she asked.

I looked at her. She was slightly disheveled and her hair was a little messed up. She looked poor. I noticed her red tennis shoes for some reason.

I didn't say anything.

"You look like Joe," she said and looked over at the service, saw all the people there. My mother came from a big family and dad had only one sister who hadn't showed. She looked back at me.

"Your father was a good man," she said and then turned, walked away.

I wanted to ask her to stop, to tell me about my father and how she knew him, but I couldn't speak.

The next day I woke early in the motel room my mother had booked for me and walked over to the office where I heard there was free coffee for the guests. I had a cup and talked to the nice lady there.

"You're with the Diggs party, right?"

"Yes," I told her.

"What did you all come up for?"

"A funeral."

"A relative?"

"Yes."

"Did you know the deceased well?"

I looked at her. "Good coffee."

"I work at the hospital next door during the week and fill in here weekend mornings. I'm an early bird. You an early bird?"

"Today I am."

"It looks like it's going to be a fine day," she said.

I looked out the window. My family had plans to meet for breakfast at a local diner in a couple of hours. I finished my coffee and said goodbye to her. I'd eaten two of the codeine pills Stacy had given me the day before. I went back, packed, ate the remaining pills.

It was a four hour drive back, there was time to think. I lit a joint somewhere in Sullivan County and looked out at the state park going by. The sun shone down on the road, the forest was densely packed pine and it looked like night between the trunks. After the burial service, we had piled over to Aunt Joyce's house. There was food, talk and drink. The Catholic priest drank bourbon, neat. I wished my radio worked. I daydreamed about having money, a place of my own. I thought about the band – we really were quite different than anyone else. It was extraordinary how we had developed our own style over the years. But I knew we would never make it. We were too poor and too volatile.

I stopped in Lewisburg for smokes and iced tea at a 7-Eleven. The cashier looked like a college chick.

"You in a band?" she asked.

"No, just passing through."

A fly was buzzing around my head.

"Looks like you got a friend," she said.

I paid her and left. The fly followed me out into the parking lot. I grabbed it out of the air and threw it on the ground, stomped on it. I was a kung fu motherfucker.

That night, Cindy went out with Stacy and I went over to Sandman's. He lived in the rooming house that Nick used to live in. We went way back. He was a record collector, had a huge collection of obscure psychedelic '60s music, mostly 45's. I beat on his back door around eight.

"Hey! Tony! Long time no see, come on in."

I pulled out a joint and lit it, handed it to him. He took a hit and the phone rang. He answered and talked while we passed the joint. Sandman had put out the Psychedelic Forgotten, which were compilation records of various obscure '60s bands. The last I heard, he was working on volume three. Sandman worked in a scrap yard part time.

He hung up the phone and said, "Yes!"

"What?"

"Man, I just sold a rare record to this guy in France for two thousand dollars!"

"What?" I handed him the joint back and he took a good hit.

"Man, you don't know," he told me. "I've been really busy. Have a record auction in Goldmine Magazine right now."

He handed me the mag and I looked at his *The Sandman Presents* auction posting, listing all the records and the starting bids. I looked at him. He nodded, smiled, and ran over to his stereo and played it for me.

"It's the only copy in the world. An acetate, a test pressing. It's on *Psychedelic Forgotten, Volume 1.*"

I remembered the song. Ward 81 would later cover the song on one of their albums. I thought, that's what geniuses do, have the world come to them.

"This calls for a celebration," Sandman said and got a box from under his bed.

I asked him what he had and he explained that the guy who lived upstairs worked as a janitor at the hospital. He emptied the trash and collected the empty morphine and Demerol bottles and gave them to Sandman for almost nothing. He emptied the box on the bed. There must have been eighty little bottles there.

"He gave me these for five bucks," Sandman said and then nodded like a crazy person.

"They're empty," I said.

"They're not. There's always something left. We just have to pry off the tops and get it out."

It was true. There was a lot left. We went through the bottles, prying the tops off with pliers, sucking it up into syringes a bit at a time. Sandman liked the Demerol and gave me the morphine bottles. We did four big shots each and there was still some left. We decided to leave the rest and walked over to the gas station to get sodas. It was a brilliant night, clear and not too hot. I wanted to walk around but he couldn't wait to get back to play more records for me. We went back. He asked me how Wendy was and I told him.

"That's cool you left her. She had you pussy-whipped."

"I didn't notice at the time."

"Yeah, well. It was pretty obvious."

"So I've heard. I'm living with some other girl now at her mother's place."

"Man. Women are evil," he said.

We smoked some more weed and he played DJ between answering the phone. "I'm going to make a killing!" he said. We joked and laughed. He told me more about selling records, how he didn't really need his job, but did it for tax purposes. I told him about the band and living in the dollhouse but didn't tell him about the love triangle. I left around midnight and he said that the guy upsatiars was going to keep bringing the bottles, that he'd save the morphine for me.

12

On Sunday I lay in bed with Cindy for most of the morning. She babbled on about what she did the night before but didn't ask what I did. I wasn't really listening anyway, was still a little high. Opiates made me feel whole and the rest of the time I just felt scattered.

"You're beautiful," I told her.

"I know."

"What?"

"A girl knows things, you know." She rubbed my chest. "You."

"What?"

"You and your what."

"I love you," I said.

She stopped rubbing my chest and dropped back on her pillow.

"Let's not go there," she said.

"I'm going to make you my muse."

"What's that?"

"You and your what. A muse is someone an artist writes about or paints. I'm going to get inside you and put all your Cindys together in a song or two. I'll assassinate you."

"Oh, god. Okay, I love you."

"Too late, I'm going to do it. I've done it before."

"You're a twisted bastard."

"I'm going to fuck you."

"All right."

She grabbed the rails at the top of her bed. It wasn't making love at all. I slammed into her and watched her gulp for air. I felt evil. She didn't love me, I was the houseboy. She faked an orgasm and I continued. She screamed. I got tired and pulled out. I couldn't come. She kissed me lightly and went to take a shower.

I lay there for a bit then went into Lois's room; she was lying there in bed. I put my cock into her mouth and she sucked it hungrily. She stopped for a second and told me she loved me.

"It's going around," I told her. "I'm going to fuck you."

"Your cock tastes like pussy," she said and went back down on me.

"When you get done sucking your daughter's juice off me, I'm gonna fuck you."

I thought she would be repulsed but she sucked harder and started playing with her pussy.

I pulled out of her mouth and got it in. She wrapped her legs around my back and told me things about feeling so wondrously dirty, so alive. She pushed me off and told me she wanted it from behind, that she never had it like that. I obliged while she bit the pillow. I made long, slow, shallow strokes. I toyed with her and took my time; she moaned and cussed a bit. I picked up the pace and made deep thrusts every once in a while. Then she started making growling noises.

Cindy poked her head in the door after her shower and I saw her.

"The houseboy is fucking your mom!" I yelled, and made a particularly deep thrust.

Lois looked over at her with the pillow in her mouth. "Gurrrr!" she said. I slapped her ass and began really pounding into her. The pillow dropped from her mouth and she said, "Ghhaaaarrrr. Rup! Rup!"

"Holy shit!" Cindy said and slammed the door.

"Oh, god," Lois said. "I'm going to come. OH. GOD! Gaaarrrrrrr, rup-rup, ieee!"

I had a hellish orgasm, poured cum into Lois. She really got loud. She came and came. Juice was running down her legs and pooling on the bed. We collapsed and lay there for a while, catching our breath.

"That was great," she finally said.

We heard the downstairs door slam. Lois giggled. "Cindy is having another tantrum," she said in a singsong voice.

We lay there for a long time in the pool of cum. Then she said we must get up. She stripped the sheets off the bed, threw them on the floor. We took a shower together and I fucked her again. More animal noises. We fucked until the water ran cold. We got out and dried off.

"I feel crazy!" she said, spinning around in the middle of the bathroom. She grabbed a glass on the sink and squatted over it. "Look, Tony, my love!" She grunted and my cum ran into the glass. Then she rubbed herself and ejaculated into the glass.

"Jesus Christ!" I said. I had never seen that much juice coming out of a woman. She moaned and kept coming. Her knees started to shake. Then she fell back on her ass, reached out and picked up the glass with both hands. There was light streaming in from the skylight, she held the glass up in the light for a moment and mumbled some words. Then she looked directly into my eyes and drank.

I brushed my teeth and combed my hair, looking at her in the mirror. She was sitting with her back to the wall, legs spread and a dazed look in her eyes. I turned to say something, but decided against it. It was possible she really was crazy and had descended into a catatonic state. There was a twisted smile frozen on her face. More cum was dripping out of her and making a little pool on the floor between her legs.

I went into Cindy's room, packed my clothes into my suitcase, took it into Lois's room and got dressed. Then I went downstairs and made coffee. A half hour or so went by. I smoked a joint outside on the patio. There was one of those round tables with the umbrella in the middle. I drank my coffee and tried to think of a song to write about Cindy but couldn't come up with anything. I made a mental note to bring my guitar over after practice, just in case I got an idea.

I went back inside and made a sandwich, put a pickle on the side, grabbed a bag of potato chips, went into the living room and turned on the TV. I clicked through the channels and settled on bowling while I ate. When I was done eating I got another cup of coffee and made some phone calls. Lonnie and Nick. Then I called Sandman and asked him.

"Yeah, come on over," he said. "There's probably four good shots apiece left."

"I'll be over soon," I told him and hung up.

I poured a cup of coffee for Lois and took it up to her. She was still sitting on the bathroom floor.

"Lois?"

"Yes?"

"You think maybe you could get up off the floor and get dressed now?"

She looked at me funny-like, and then looked at the puddle between her legs. She slapped it and giggled. She put her hands into it and rubbed it all over her tits and belly. She rubbed it on her face and into her hair.

"Am I pretty?" she asked me.

"You're beautiful. Now cut it out, you're making a mess."

"You're my man now."

"Yes, Lois."

"I'm your woman." She put her fingers into her mouth and licked them.

I started getting hard again. I turned on the shower and got her in there, got her toweled off and she drank the coffee.

"Hmmm... Where were we?" she asked.

"Look, I have to go out. Do you want me to make you some lunch?"

"No, I'll get something. You'll come back soon?"

I told her I'd be back in a few hours and she said she would make us a fine dinner.

* * * * *

It was around six when I got back from Sandman's. We had done the last of his morphine and listened to records. I smelled food and went into the kitchen. Lois was dressed in a black silk slip and had her fuzzy pink slippers on.

"Hello, lover," she said as I walked into the room. She had dark red lipstick smeared on her lips and had overdone the perfume.

"Hello, lover," I replied and grabbed her around the waist, kissed her. "God, you smell great and the food smells great. Where's Cindy?"

"She called, said she was freaked out about us. Said she was spending the night at Stacy's. Whatever, I'm glad she's out of our hair for the night."

I let her go and leaned on the counter. I was really stoned.

"Tony?"

"Yes?"

"Could you be a dear and make me a drink? The roast is almost ready."

She handed me the glass and I took it out to the living room, filled her glass with scotch. "Make one for yourself too!" she yelled.

Nope, caffeine. I took her the drink and got a bottle of Coke from the fridge, poured myself one and added ice.

"You want ice?" I asked her.

"No ice."

She swilled down her drink and told me to make her another.

We had dinner at the dining room table. Roast beef, mashed potatoes and gravy, green beans. I picked at it. She was wolfing the food down and chasing it with scotch after scotch. Her talk got looser and looser. She was an animal; I had turned her into an animal.

"What the hell are you looking at?" she asked with her mouth full.

I didn't say anything, just wanted to lie on some couch somewhere. Just wanted to drink Coke with ice cubes.

That night was an aberration, a surreal meat game. The dolls watched us from the shadows.

13

Before we knew it, it was July. Lois had told me to quit my job soon after I moved into her room and I did. It was a bad idea. I started looking for another job after a week of it. There was a stint at the local temp agency where you never knew where you'd be sent, day to day. I moved furniture, worked in scrap yards sorting scrap metal and then spent a few weeks as the mascot for Monk's Furniture, standing outside in a chipmunk costume, waving at the cars driving by. I kind of liked that job; it was ridiculous. I danced and waved. I shook my ass at the street and jumped up and down. I had a pipe hidden around the side of the building and did one-hitters all day long.

That job came to an end one day when some drunk rednecks piled out of a truck and came at me. I danced and weaved, called them queer for the chipmunk. I was the only kung fu motherfucking chipmunk in the world.

"The customer is always right!" Monk told me when he dismissed me.

I heard the same thing from my boss at the temp agency.

"Look; I can send you back to the scrap yard tomorrow," he said.

"Nah, thanks but no."

"Did you really kick three guys' asses in Monk's parking lot?"

"They were begging for it."

He looked at me. He was old. Like thirty-five or something. He looked puzzled.

"You should have seen me, man," I explained. "I did a little dance, said, nobody fucks with the chipmunk!" I showed him the dance.

He laughed lightly and then groaned, leaned his elbows on his desk and rubbed his face, looked back at me. "You don't belong here, Tony," he finally said.

14

Then I was at the beach with Lois and she was explaining how Cape May was one of the oldest resorts in the country. That presidents and other famous people went there in the 1800's. We walked around town and she pointed out this and that landmark, this and that Victorian building. "My parents brought me here as a child and I've been coming every summer since," she said.

My parents had never taken us to the beach, every summer it was upstate to the grandparents' house and the dead weight of family. Later on, there were some cool trips though. Up to Maine, over to the Thousand Islands in the St. Lawrence Seaway. Down to Skyline Drive in Virginia, my dad got out of the car to take a picture of a bear and mom said, "Joe! Get back in the damn car!" He ignored her and crept up to the bear, got the picture. Bear digging in trash can – a man's art - a moment of bravery and abandon. I laughed thinking of this.

"What?" Lois said.

"Oh, nothing."

"Are you stoned?"

"No."

"You know, I'm not a prude about drugs. You seem to handle yourself well, not let it get out of hand."

"What would you know about it?"

"I knew some bohemian types in college, way back in the late '50s. Poets and artists. Wine and weed types."

"You ever get high with them?"

"No. I was the straight girl, we weren't really friends. But I went to a few of their poetry readings and art exhibits. To be honest, I envied them, their freedom. Then I met Bob. I was pregnant with Cindy by our senior year."

She looped her arm in mine and we walked along. It was a beautiful day, pretty people all around. She told me there was a nature reserve to the south of Cape May that ran to the tip of New Jersey.

"Want to go there?" I asked.

"No, let's have drinks." She steered me into a bar called The Ugly Mug. I was going to say something about it being a little early but didn't. She ordered scotch and soda since we were out. I knew it would be straight scotch later, in the hotel room. I ordered rum and Coke. She paid. That was the deal. She was to pay for everything.

"Do you think Cindy will be all right?" I asked her.

"Oh, she'll get over it. It's good to see you two getting along better."

"I think she's sweet." I wanted them both. I wanted a harem but didn't say it.

"She's a little manipulator. You know, she has a college degree in accounting. I sent her to Penn State for four years."

"Really? I didn't know that."

"Oh, yes. Graduated near the top of her class. After graduation... Bartender? Could I have another?"

The bartender got her another drink and she asked me if I wanted another.

"I'm good. I could dig some food though."

He brought us menus and went back to watching TV. We were the only ones in the bar. She pushed her menu aside and lit a smoke, offered me one and lit it for me.

"After graduation she got a good job in Carlisle as a bookkeeper. She moved out for a while, a couple of years. Had a nice apartment and then started running with the wrong crowd. There's nothing you can do, right? You try to bring them up right and give them everything thinking they're better than all the other kids, but they don't care. They come back to you telling you some boyfriend beat them up and they lost their job. They're a mess. They stay knowing you love them, that you won't kick them out."

"What happened?"

"I don't know, Tony. She's been with me ever since. You shoulda seen some of the guys she came home with.

Then there was the cancer and now here we are."

A couple came into the bar and got beers. They looked over at us. I ordered a cheeseburger and fries and Lois got another drink. I got a Coke. Lois lit another cigarette.

"We must look like a funny couple," Lois said.

I didn't say anything, sipped my Coke and thought about heroin.

"They probably think I'm your mom," she whispered in my ear and giggled.

"Cut it out, Lois."

"Oh, I'm sorry. I didn't mean anything. Come to think of it, I never asked about your family. God, but I'm such a lush."

"That's all right," I told her.

"No. You must tell me."

"I can't. I can't talk about it. Please don't ask."

"Oh, a sore spot, eh? All right. I tell you and you don't tell me anything. I see how it works."

"Maybe later," I told her as the food came.

I ate and she drank. After I ate I played a few games of pool with some guys that had come in. Lois sat at the bar. One of the guys asked me about her, saying she was hot.

"She used to be a model," I told him. "Met her last night up in Wildwood."

I kicked everyone's ass at the pool table and went back to her as night fell. She had been buying us drinks the whole time. I had a big chunk of hash and had been slipping into the bathroom and outside to take hits the whole afternoon.

She had a crowd of guys around her by that time, buying her drinks. Musclemen and guys my age. Beach bums. I edged my way between them and told her we were leaving. She didn't want to go. I waited...

The beginning of the week was like this. I eventually

just left her there in the early afternoon and went to the beach. I bodysurfed. I met some folks my age and we hung out all day. In the evening I would go collect the remnants of Lois. We'd have dinner someplace and go back to the hotel. She'd drink and I'd smoke hash on the balcony. We'd talk. Then we'd fuck and she'd pass out. I'd sit on the balcony smoking more hash, looking at the ocean 'til early morning.

Thursday night she decided she wanted to try some hash.

"Are you sure?" I asked.

"Yes. I want to know what it's all about. It smells sweet; I like the smell of it."

I loaded the bowl and handed it to her, lit it. She took a hit and blew it out.

"Not like that, Lois. You have to hold the smoke in your lungs for as long as you can. It's not like smoking cigarettes."

"I think I feel it."

"Trust me, you don't feel it. If it's really your first time it'll probably take a few bowls to get you high."

"Really?"

"Yes."

"I'm going to get another drink," she said.

"No. No drink. Have a Coke with me and try this first. Then see if you want another drink, okay?"

"Well, all right. I'm a little scared. You'll protect me if I have a bad trip?"

"Ha! Relax. It's not like that but, yes, I'll protect you."

She got up and went to the little refrigerator, got a Coke and came back out. She had the black silk slip on again with nothing underneath. I was in my old undershorts. Nobody could see us up there on the balcony; it was just ocean, sky and us.

"God, but you're a sexy woman," I told her.

"Why, thank you dear," she said. "I'm going to fuck you soon."

"I'm going to fuck you."

"No, me fucking, you fuckee. I want the top tonight. It's a great night, look at the stars!"

"Now, where were we? Let's have that bowl again."

I lit it for her and she smoked the whole thing. I re-loaded it and took a good hit for myself and told her to smoke the rest. "Yes, like that," I told her. She was getting it right, holding in the hits 'til she coughed.

It really was a beautiful night. The smell of the ocean blended with the smell of hashish and Lois's perfume. I got another slice of the pizza we had brought back with us and another Coke while she worked on the bowl.

"Mmm; it tastes luscious," she said, and took another hit, held it in.

It was incredible fortune, meeting Cindy and her. Even with the houseboy gigolo garbage, it was way better than the life I had been leading. I looked out at the vast ocean and thought how much clarity it brought. Clarity and even serenity. I smelled the air and ate my pizza. Then she was finished with the bowl. She handed it to me and lit a cigarette.

"It didn't work, I think I need more," she said.

"Wait a bit, Lois. Drink your Coke. God, what a night! Look at the ocean! It's massive and wet. Did you ever look at it and think about Europe, just on the other side? About this ball we live on that spins through space? It's really odd and fine to be alive. I feel really good. Isn't it all grand?"

She didn't say anything.

I looked at her. She was looking out at the ocean. "Lois?"

She giggled lightly and kept staring into space.

Friday, she went to the beach with me. I tried to talk her

into going in the water but she didn't want to. "I'll watch you," she said. I bodysurfed and poked my head out of some waves as they came in. I waved at her and played the clown. I could see her laughing and kept doing it. Then we laid on her beach towel under an umbrella she had rented.

"I feel so different, Tony. I don't know what to do," she said.

"Want to go back to our room and get high?"

"No, we can do that later. I need a drink."

"No you don't. Let's lay here a while. Look at all the pretty people. What the hell do they do anyway? Who the hell are they?"

She turned over and wrapped her leg around my waist, rubbed my chest and stuck her tongue in my ear. We went back and fucked with abandon then went to the bar. That night, we got high again and she said she just wanted me to hold her, that she didn't want to have sex. I told her all right and we lay there for a long while, snuggling. Then she got out of bed, pulled on her robe and went out on the balcony. After a bit, I went out there. We sat looking at the night ocean, not saying a word.

Saturday night after Lois had passed out, I took the long walk through the reserve to the southern tip of New Jersey. It seemed like everything was about to change, that things were almost done playing themselves out. It seemed like a good place to sit for awhile; a good place to think. I looked up at the sky and picked out some constellations and remembered doing that on Nick's roof, years earlier. He had built a platform up there and we would smoke weed and look. Later on, we built a grand tree fort in my parents' backyard. It was way up in a big old locust; the floor was thirty feet above the ground. We had a radio up there that picked up stations hundreds of miles away on clear nights. We brought up our guitars and played. It really was a massive structure, the crowning achievement of all the forts we had built in the woods since we were kids.

We had stolen all the wood for the thing from the local building sites that had been springing up and turning our fields and woods into suburbs. It was our turf. We couldn't stop them, but we could steal.

I remembered hotwiring a steam roller one night and running it into the walls of some new house. We wrecked that place and put the steam roller in a ditch. But we couldn't stop them. The developers came and came. They swallowed the woods and the Indian ghosts went off somewhere else. I wanted to cry about it. I wanted to cry for my father. But I had grown cold and warlike. Vengeful.

There was probably something there to see that night on the tip of New Jersey. Something about the world spinning me at the nexus of the Delaware and Atlantic; something earthy and magical. But I couldn't see it.

Driving back the next day, Lois said, "I have something to tell you," from the passenger seat.

I didn't say anything, just drove.

"Tony?"

"Yes?"

"I'm, ah... Well... Do you love me?"

"Yeah, sure."

"No you don't."

"I like you."

"I like you too," she said.

"Everything's Archie."

"What?"

"Never mind."

"Look, I need you to promise me something."

"What's that, Lois?"

"I have to go away for a while, so I need you to stay

with Cindy. She can't be alone, you know."

"What makes you think I would leave?"

"Men always leave."

"Where are you going?"

"Oh god, I feel foolish. I've been such a fool."

"Join the crowd."

"Ha! That's what I like about you, Tony. Always seeing the funny side of things. Well, I guess it is kind of funny... I'm going into rehab. This was my last big party week and I spent it with you and I'm glad I did. You have been kind and patient."

"For my next trick I become a gigolo. A real one this time though."

She ignored me and went on. "I'm being forced into it. In case you didn't know, I've been drinking quite a bit more than I let on. The people I work with confronted me about it. I've been drinking almost as much at work as at home. I suppose it got obvious. They gave me an ultimatum."

She looked out the window and started crying.

"Oh no, not that. Everything's gonna be all right," I said, thinking that it probably wasn't. That it was a pretty stupid thing to say.

"I've felt so different with you, Tony. So alive. And now, I'm afraid of everything. I'm afraid of losing you, afraid I never really had you, that nobody ever really has anybody. I'm afraid for Cindy and wonder what's going to become of her. I'M AFRAID OF DYING, TONY!" she sobbed.

I really didn't know what to say, just drove on, stone-faced. She sobbed some more and then cleared her throat.

"I'm sorry."

"That's all right," I told her. "I'm sorry that I don't know what to say. I'll say that I think it's true. Nobody ever does really have anybody. Life is almost too sad to bear. You must be stubborn, you must laugh, get mean. Hell, I dunno."

We drove on in silence for a while.

"Two months," she said. "I'll be away for two months. I've instructed my lawyer to pay the bills and to make sure there's food in the refrigerator. He's to continue Cindy's allowance, which is fifty dollars a week. I've also instructed him to pay you a hundred dollars a week for house-sitting and just being there."

A year earlier I would have said no, keep your money. A year ago I would have been honorable and brave. But I had learned. I drove on up toward Vineland.

15 Redemption House was located on a sunny side street on the outskirts of Scranton. Lois looked at the brochure and the map as I drove.

"Hey, this car handles nicely," I told her as I swung up through some curves on 81.

She didn't say anything, just looked at me and smiled.

"BM double youuu!" I said. "You, you, youuuu!" I stomped on it, hit ninety, blew past a few cars.

"Take it easy, Tony."

"All right."

"Thanks for trying to cheer me up."

"Oh, I wasn't..."

"Yes you were; that's what you do. You like to entertain."

"I do?"

"You like playing the clown. I think it's because you're hiding something. It's a diversion."

I didn't say anything. We went up into the mountains.

"It's all right to hurt, you know. It's all right to share things with friends," she said and touched my arm. I drove for a bit.

"You're preparing yourself for what's in store, huh? Psychology stuff?"

"Yes. That's possible."

"What about the law of the jungle? Enemies will prey on any perceived weakness."

"What enemies?"

I didn't say anything.

"Oh hell, Tony."

"I'm not evil, but I'm mean. I've done some mean things to survive."

"You are not mean. Let's not talk about it. Let's just relax and enjoy the drive."

I drove on and we didn't say much. The day before

was spent mostly in bed. We smoked hash and she drank the last of her scotch. My nuts were like raisins.

We got there and parked. I took her bags and we went in. The nurse at the front desk took a good look at us as we walked up.

"Hello," Lois said to the nurse.

"What is his name?" she asked.

"My name is Lois Williams. I'm the one checking in."

"Oh, I'm sorry! I just thought…" She looked flustered as she paged through her pad. "Here you are, Miss Williams," she said.

"Mrs. Williams," Lois corrected.

She took another look at me and then looked back at Lois. Her confusion had made her angry. She looked like the type that needed to get angry to get anything done.

"I'll page the orderly and he'll come get your bags and take you up," she said coolly. "Could I have your insurance card?"

Lois handed her the card and rolled her eyes at me.

"Just give us the room number and I'll take her up," I told her.

"Oh, I'm sorry. Mister?"

"Mister Diggs."

"Mister Diggs. I'm sorry but there are to be no visitors to the rooms. It's Redemption House policy."

"Policy just changed," I told her.

"Oh, please excuse Mr. Diggs. He's very protective of me," Lois said and grabbed my arm. She pulled me out of the place and into the parking lot.

"Don't make a scene, Tony. Just let me go."

I kissed her and she pushed me away.

"I'll come up every weekend. Visiting times are weekend afternoons, right?"

"Yeah, that's what they say. But you don't have to

come. In fact, please don't. I have to go through this alone."

"I'll be here," I said, but both of us knew I wouldn't.

We walked back in and several orderlies were there in starched white uniforms. I had my arm around her waist and held her hands.

"Is there going to be a problem?" one of the orderlies asked us. The nurse at the front desk looked alive, like she wanted to see blood, my blood. I sized up the orderlies. Big, like nightclub bouncers. I was ready...

"TONY!" Lois said. "It's all right honey, let me go. I'll be all right."

I stared at them all. "You take good care of her. You take care," I said stupidly. I wanted to kill them. I wanted to rip their guts out and stomp them into the nice carpet. I wanted to...

"Let me go, honey. You're hurting my hands."

I let her go and she walked off with the boys in white.

"That's my friend," I heard her say. She turned and waved. The doors closed. I stood there looking at the doors. Then I looked at the desk nurse. Then I went out to her car, started it and drove off.

For some reason I remembered Plymouth as I drove south. I pulled off the interstate at Wilkes-Barre and stopped, looked at the map. I knew it was around there somewhere. I knew what it was – they had been passing around pictures after my father's burial at my aunt's house. Whatever they call the after-burial get-together was there. Food and drink. People. Talk. There were some pictures of him, his sister and my grandparents as a child and I had turned one of the pictures over and seen *Plymouth, PA - 1915*, written on the back. I found it on the map and drove over in Lois's car.

It was a small town built on the side of a mountain just across the river from Wilkes-Barre. I drove past the Plymouth Works, the old coal mine, and wished I could kill the people that ran it a hundred years ago. All the years of driving upstate to visit family as a kid, we had never been there. My father never spoke of it but my mother told me that his father got black lung in those mines, that he started work there when he was still a child.

"It was way before the child labor laws," she told me one day in our backyard when I was a kid. It was one of those odd summer days when school was out and my friends were off somewhere. I was bored and was helping her clean the storm windows before she repainted them to store away for the next winter. Dad was at work. I asked her when they moved to Waverly and she said she didn't know, that my father didn't talk much about it.

"His parents died a long time ago," she said. "I never met them. Go get the hose. We have to wash the soap off these things. I have to start dinner soon."

I drove around Plymouth and up into the hills, looking for the house from the picture. They all looked alike. I pulled up next to a small decrepit house that was on the outskirts of the town and stopped the car. It wasn't the house; it didn't matter. The road dead-ended and turned to a dirt trail that went up the side of the mountain. My grandfather walked with my father up the trail...

16

It really had gotten bad for us – very few gigs and the ones we got didn't pay squat. The playlists kept coming in the mail. Wendy would put them in an envelope and slip them under the door of our rehearsal room. It seemed we were known everywhere but in our home town. One day Nick asked if he went to the city and got some shit together for us, would I move up? I told him I would, thinking nothing would come of it. We were losers, born of losers and meant to carry on the tradition. But then he was holding an NYC sign and walking up 6th St. I pulled over and gave him a ride to the highway.

Lonnie and I moved all our gear up to his place after he left and I told the guys in Blacklisted they could have our practice room. Phil, the leader of Blacklisted, came to meet me there and I gave him the key. I gave him the address to send the check to.

"Don't I need to meet the landlord?"

"Hell, Phil - this is how I got the room. I never met the guy; he's a doctor, owns the office upstairs. You can't play anytime before five on weekdays and you can't live here."

"Cool," he said. "Thanks. Hey, we're thinking of putting out a record but don't know how to go about it."

I told him what I knew, thought about charging them for my college radio contact list but didn't. It had been given to me free of charge by Sandman.

I got into a somber mood after all that had happened and quit everything. Quit smoking and drinking, cut out all drugs. Tim, Lois's lawyer, came Fridays to pick up the bills and give Cindy and I our allowance. The first time he came he told me he didn't much care to go food shopping for us. Cindy just looked at the money and went to her room to make some phone calls. I looked at him – failed attempt at sportscaster's hair, old suit and fighting a potbelly. He looked haggard.

"Look, Tim. I was led to understand you had an agreement with Lois about all this, that we would give you a list and you would go shopping for us."

"Well... Lois. I guess I just can't say no to her."

He looked around the room, a turtle out of his shell. Life had murdered him somehow. Lois had murdered him, strung him along.

"Just throw me an extra hundred a week and I'll take care of it," I told him.

"I don't know. I'm to give Lois a weekly report."

"Just tell her it's been taken care of. I'll clear it with her, she trusts me."

"You're sure?"

"She told you, right?"

"Yes, Tony. She told me."

It was pitiful.

He peeled off five twenties and gave them to me. "What you don't need you'll return to me next Friday, right? She has me on a tight budget."

It was worse than I thought. I told him yes and led him to the door.

He reached out his hand and I shook it.

"Well, I guess this is..." he started and I slammed the door in his face.

Cindy had started hanging out with coke freaks. They piled into the living room nightly, snorting lines, drinking, smoking weed. She started fucking Dwayne, who brought the coke. There was no place to hide, nothing to do. I stayed in Lois's room, playing my guitar and smelling her scent on the pillow.

I think I will leave you here, leave the blind, stoned pilot in your car. Waxed and beyond rebellion. I will lean out windows and stand on sidewalks bleeding out centuries. I will be anonymous, a blood-filled ghost, a walking corpse, my jaw will flop as a door loose on its hinge, in the wind that blows…

The door flung open.

"Tony!" It was Cindy.

"What?"

"Didn't you hear me calling you? The phone! Pick up the phone!"

She slammed the door shut and I heard, "Tony!" from downstairs. They laughed. "Tony's a monk!" I heard Dwayne say. Everyone roared laughter.

I picked up the phone.

"Tony?"

"Nick?"

"Yeah, man! How you been?"

"Things been a bit funny. Man! It's good to hear your voice!"

"I'm living in this place in the East Village. It's great here, man! The people are cool! Fuck. You guys didn't replace me, did you?"

Later that night Cindy came into the room explaining that she kicked everyone out early. She crawled onto the bed with me.

"What are you doing?" she asked.

"Nothing. Laying here. Where's Dwayne?"

"Oh, he went off somewhere for a few days. Philadelphia, I think. I heard you playing your guitar earlier. Did you ever write any songs about me?"

"I tried but they wouldn't come."

"Tony?"

"Yes?"

"I didn't do any coke tonight, just drank."

"You done with your latest binge?"

"I don't know. I was going to do some and something inside told me to wait, to look at them. So that's what I did. It didn't look pretty like it feels when you're on the stuff and babbling."

"You thought you were looking at them, but you were looking at yourself."

"Oh, you know?"

"It's hard."

She sighed and lay back on the bed.

"I can't lie here with you. Come to my room," she said and got up, left.

I got up and went into her room.

"You aren't mad at me any more?" I asked.

"It was too much work."

"What are we going to do?"

She took off her clothes and got into her bed. "I'm going to fuck you," she said. "Who knows what will happen later?"

I took off my clothes and got into bed. She got on top and rode me 'til I hardened. Then she had me inside her. I wanted to master her, to master the physical world, but knew it wasn't with me. I was only the master of fleeting musical moments and theater of the streets. She seemed to sense my mood and slowed her pace.

Later that night, I dreamt I was flying over the Harrisburg skyline. As soon as I found I could control my flight I was instantly flying upstate, over the mountains. I soared and dived. Then I was flying down the avenues of Manhattan. I stopped to light on the roof of a building, I was a gargoyle. I screamed like I imagined pterodactyls did. There was a guitar cord that plugged the tracheotomy incision in my throat into the building. What came out was a monstrously loud, obscene, fuzz-soaked howl. People on the streets below screamed and ran, cars wrecked into buildings, into each other. I did it again...

In the morning I took my suitcase back into her room and looked at all the dolls. They seemed to be sleeping.

"We have a gig in New York City next month," I told her.

"Are you going to take me with you?"
"Who knows what will happen?" I said.

17

Mickey Luther ran with the Yippies in the '60s. He went on to Amsterdam in the '70s and fell in with the remnants of the Dutch Provo movement, who denounced work and called for social rebellion. By the time Mickey was deported by the Dutch authorities, he was running one of the biggest retail pot operations in Europe. He went back to the Lower East Side of Manhattan, started the Church of Realized Fantasies and declared himself Pope. The guy had legal papers drawn up saying it was a real church, that marijuana was the sacrament. The cops couldn't do anything about it. Not that the cops cared, they had enough problems with wide scale heroin traffic in the neighborhood.

After a while, the Church's business skyrocketed. There were lines of cars going around the block, Mickey had runners going out selling eighth bags to them, kids that had no homes, nothing. They were bringing the weed in and taking the money out in trash bags.

The local Puerto Rican gang called the Hitman Club confronted Mickey on the street one day, demanding protection money. Mickey told them to fuck off and they promptly pulled guns and blew six rounds into him. A small riot broke out on 11th St.; the people from the Church came out and fought with the Ricans. They dragged Mickey back into the Church. Mickey was so pissed and so fat that he didn't feel anything. But somebody took him to the hospital as night fell. The Hitman Club came pouring into the building, took some kids hostage. That night, the Hitman Club did a bunch of heroin and nodded out downstairs. The fire marshal decided it was a dropped cigarette that started the fire.

Nick was there that night with a guy named Choo-Choo. They escaped over the rooftops. Choo-Choo started a delivery service after the Church collapsed.

"You're being so quiet. What are you thinking?" Cindy

asked. We had just finished breakfast and were sitting on the couch.

"The gig. We have a thirty minute slot to fill and I was thinking about the set list." It was a lie. I was actually thinking about what Nick had said, that he could get me a job in the city doing what he did, being a pot messenger, that business was going crazy and Choo wanted to give me a job. This was the plan we had talked about for so long, a plan I had gone along with thinking it would never happen, that I wasn't ready, would never be ready for anything big, that the world would crush me at any given moment. So I just lived day to day with no real ideas, just make-believe plans to bolster make-believe courage.

"I worked on my painting again last night after you fell asleep. Want to see it?"

"Sure, let's have a look," I said and we went into the back room where she had her little studio. She had been dabbling with painting off and on for years. Lois encouraged her. She had been working on this particular piece for many months.

"See?" she said.

I looked at it, didn't see anything different. It was a painting of a city street scene with people and buildings and cars. As a realist, she wasn't so good. It seemed like she wanted it to look like a picture and I wondered why she didn't just take photos.

"I like this color. The brain wants to define it as blue or green, but fails," I said, like a professor.

"It's teal," she said. "You don't really see what I did, do you?"

"No."

"I erased some people and put you and me in there."

"Where?"

"Here!" she pointed. It didn't look like us at all.

"That's nice," I said, and she stomped off upstairs. I looked at it again and then followed her up.

"I'm not like you, Tony! I can't just wing it all the time like you do! That's not art, art takes time and suffering! You don't get it, man!"

I didn't get it.

"Didn't you ever want to just spill it?" I asked her.

"What do you mean?"

"You know, just go crazy with it. Spill out all your psychoses, nightmares and beautiful dreams, just go crazy with it?"

"I'm not crazy!"

Then I got into an argument about art and psychology with the girl who had a degree in accounting and lived with her mother. I took my car and drove off.

There was nothing to do and no place to go. I wanted so much, but my world was too small. I started having a crisis: I should get a job, I shoulda married Wendy, I shoulda stayed in college, what the hell am I doing living in the dollhouse anyway? Do you love Cindy or Lois? Yes. No. I ended up at my mother's house after driving around for an hour or so. I sat there looking at the house and imagining some conversation:

"Anthony! What are you doing here?" my mother asked.

"Hiya mom. Can I come in?"

"Well, yes. Sure," she said and let me in. "We all thought you were dead. You never come over or call. Have a seat. There's some coffee left if you want some."

"Yeah, I'll take some coffee. You sit, I'll get it."

I went into the kitchen and poured a cup. Added milk. Went back into the living room.

Mom was standing there, looking at me. "You look really healthy."

"I'm doing okay. How are you holding up?"

"Oh, I manage," she said.

I put my cup down and hugged her, told her I was sorry I never came over.

"Oh, that's all right. You're young and busy," she said. "Sit down. We'll catch up."

I walked over to my father's chair and then walked past it and sat in the other chair. "Good coffee," I said.

"Your father made better. He was always up before me, always made the coffee."

We were silent for a bit. I looked around the room, it seemed different. "I guess Ann's at work?"

"Yeah, she's at work. You're not working again?"

"No. Well I have a job house-sitting. Some people I met through my band went to Europe for the summer and I'm staying at their house, cutting the lawn and stuff. It's over in Melrose Gardens."

"Melrose Gardens? Rich folks?"

"Yeah, I suppose. It's not much of a job; I'm used to hard work all day. It's a bit ridiculous, to be honest."

"They're paying you?"

"Oh, yeah. I stay there for free and they pay me on top of it."

She laughed. "Only you would come up with a scam like that. Ha! Rich folks. You'll get tired of that quick. I know you. Growing up you could never sit still and I don't think that's changed."

"No, it hasn't changed. I'm tired of it already. You need help with anything around the house?"

"No. Your sister does the lawn and I take care of everything else. Didn't you notice the living room?"

"Oh. You painted it?"

"Yeah, it needed it. When Joe got ill, there wasn't much time to take care of things around the house."

I didn't say anything. There was a lump in my throat. I didn't belong there. I didn't belong anywhere.

"My band has a gig in New York City next month,"

I told her.

"That's fantastic!"

"Yeah, it's pretty cool. We've been working hard and it seems like it might pay off one of these days."

"Where are you playing?"

"Someplace uptown called The Hive."

"Your father took me to New York for our honeymoon."

"I didn't know that."

"There's a lot you don't know. We went to see a play on Broadway. Oh, we had a grand time. He was such a gentleman."

She looked off like she was dreaming. She smiled. "I see a lot of him in you."

"No way," I said.

"Oh, don't get angry. He loved you. Damn but you fought with us so."

"I'm sorry."

"No you're not. That's fine. I didn't know him when he was your age but I imagine that he was quite like you as you are now."

I didn't know what to say.

She looked at me and smiled. "It's okay to come over and hug your mother once in a while, okay to talk."

I saw the drapes pull back and someone looking out the window. I started my car and turned around, drove back up the dead end street.

I see a lot of him in you.

Don't get angry.

18

I drove back to the dollhouse and called Lonnie. He asked if it was still on for the weekend, if Nick was still coming down. I told him yes.

"Look man, it's a nice day. I'm going swimming. You want to come over?"

"What?"

"Swimming, man. In the river. I know this great place."

There was silence. Then, "Man, Lonnie don't swim."

"Oh, come on! Get your sorry ass down here."

"Nope, fuck that. Come on up later, we'll get some beer."

I told him I'd call him back that evening.

Cindy was in her room, sulking. "Get your swimsuit," I told her. "We're going swimming!"

"I need some drugs," she said.

I jumped up and down on her bed, "We're going the fuck swimming!" Boing-boing. I attempted a flip, landed on the edge, fell on the floor, sprung back up.

"He-he," she said. "Do it again."

I jumped up and down hitting my hands on the ceiling and pushing off. Boing-b-boing. I flipped and landed on my back, bounced to my knees then stood on my head. I was her magic man.

She laughed, said, "All right," and jumped out of bed.

I stripped off my jeans, dug out my cut-offs and put them on while she dug into her dresser and started comparing bikinis.

"What's gotten into you, Tony?"

"I'm crazy! Tony's gone nutso!"

"Weee! That's fine, man! Which one should I wear?"

I almost said I didn't care, but knew it would take forever. I pointed at one and she stripped, put it on. She put on some cut-off shorts and a t-shirt and we got some towels.

"I used to go to this place all the time in the summer," I told her as we drove over.

We got there and I pulled off to the side of the road.

"Where is it?"

"It's here," I told her. "Get down to your bikini. I'll show you."

She pulled off her pants and shirt. It was impossible. She should have been a model. We got out and I led her under the fence and down to the river. There was a shallow beach there, mostly dirt and pebbles. Some kids a bit younger than us were hanging there and some others were swimming around in the river. We said hi to the kids and waded in.

"It gets deeper. Let's go out to the big rock," I told her.

"They saw my scars," she said.

"Don't worry about it. You're beautiful. Nobody in their right mind would ever get to your scars, they'd be too busy looking at the rest of you."

"You think?

"Come on."

We waded out 'til it was deep enough to swim in. We swam out to the big diving rock in the middle of the river. Some people were there smoking weed. We smoked with them, dived and swam. We did the back float and the dog paddle. Seagulls flew up from the Chesapeake and circled overhead. Long-legged birds stood in the shallows, stork-like. My mom was a bird watcher, knew all their names. Egrets? Something like that. Snowy and blue. They dunked their beaks into the water for fish, billowy clouds blew overhead.

We spent all afternoon out there. The couple was our age, I looked at her crotch; she had a frontal wedgie. The guy looked at Cindy and the girls looked at each other.

We were still on the rock in the middle of the river when the sun started going down and the guy said he was going back for beer.

"Let's get naked," I said to the girls, and took off my clothes, leaving them on the big rock. I dove into the river. I came up and said, "It's not sex, it's just getting naked. You should feel how good this feels. Nobody will see us, it's almost dark."

I could see them talking to each other and giggling. I swam off upstream and forgot them, I swam and swam, then I did a back float back down stream. I lifted my head and they weren't on the rock anymore. Then I felt an arm around my waist, pulling me down. I went under water and felt pussy. We came up. It wasn't Cindy. Cindy was splashing water on us. The girl's boyfriend was back and yelling from the shore, "I got beer! Come on in!" Cindy splashed water on us. We were on the other side of the diving rock in the middle of the river. Nobody on the shore could see us.

"Come back in the water with us!" the girl yelled.

"No! I'm dry now. Quit playing around, Lucy! I got beer!"

I got my finger in Lucy and she moaned a bit. Cindy swam up to us and said, "It looks like Tony's got you. You want to fuck him?" she whispered in Lucy's ear.

"Jake's up there," she said.

"Fuck her, Tony," Cindy said.

"No. You fuck her."

Cindy swam over and got her finger in. "Yell over to Jake that we'll be in soon," she said.

"We're swimming in, Jake!" Lucy said. They played with each other's pussies and kissed.

"I've never done this before," Lucy said. "You're so beautiful."

"I'm gonna eat your pussy," Cindy said.

We swam to the rock and Lucy lay back with her legs spread and her feet in the water. I watched for a bit, then put my shorts back on and swam on in. Jake handed me a towel and a beer.

"They wanted to swim around some more," I said.

"Damnit!" he said and loaded another bowl. We smoked and drank beer. I had forgotten how sound carries across water. We heard some moans and cries.

"My girlfriend is bisexual," I explained.

"Mine isn't!"

"It doesn't mean anything, let them play. Can I have another beer?"

He gave me one, opened one for himself and sat down in the dirt. It sounded like they were really going at it.

"Ahh, that's Cindy. She always does that. That 'Uh, uh, oh yes, mmm, oh! Oh!' Always getting higher in pitch."

He looked at me. "Jesus Christ!" he said.

I laughed and yelled out. "Uh, uh, oh yes, oh! Oh!"

The sound of Cindy's laughter came back over the water.

19

It was stupid. I had been making ninety dollars a week busting my ass at the Coke plant and now was pulling in one hundred a week on top of the money Lois's lawyer gave me for food and supplies. It was the American Dream, bastardized. It was the dollhouse and all the women in it. It was suburban lawns and trash out on Mondays. It was talking to the neighbors over the fence and telling ridiculous lies: I was Lois's nephew on college break. Yes, Penn State. Uh-huh, Center County is beautiful. Go Lions! Lois is in Europe, she says hello in her postcards.

I searched myself for something honorable and thought there was still something there, some small center I hadn't forgotten. But I knew it was getting smaller. The world was flat and I was falling off the edge.

Cindy was yelling at me that we needed some things from the store.

"You go," I told her.

"Mom said you would take care of it. She obviously trusts you with the money better than me."

She was mad. I was having another crisis of conscience and didn't want to fuck her. Well, that's how it goes, you're probably a sociopath.

"Tony?"

"Yes?"

"Quit looking out the window and go to the store. I made a list."

I took Lois's car. The Muzak came in through strategically spaced speakers in the ceiling. It was maddening. I careened down the aisles and threw things in the cart.

I got back to the car after checking out. As I piled the bags into the trunk a car pulled up next to me. It was a silver Mercedes sports coupe. I pushed the cart back to the entrance of the store and walked back. The guy in the Mercedes was looking at me. He got out, said, "Hey!"

I ignored him and opened the door to get in the

car.

"Hey! I'm talking to you!" he said.

I looked at him and didn't say anything.

"What the hell are you doing?" he asked.

I looked at him, thinking, maybe this is the guy. Maybe I'll kick this guy's ass and then the rest of the day would be all right. Again, I didn't say anything, shook a cig out of the pack I had bought at the store thinking, I'd start smoking again, it would keep me away from opiates and killing people. I lit it and blew smoke at the sky. I was a Neanderthal in the flailing ends of the industrial age. We'll all go to hell and I'll drive the...

"That's my wife's car!" he said, walking over to me.

"Ah, Bob," I said. "Your ex-wife."

He looked mad. "Who the hell are you?"

I smoked. It was bad. I still wasn't a much of a smoker.

"I'm Tony," I told him, like that explained everything.

"What?"

"I'm taking care of things for Lois while she's in Europe," I told him and then got in the car and drove off. When I got back to the dollhouse I noticed the license plate: BLUVSL.

"I need some drugs," I told Cindy when I walked in with the groceries.

She mumbled something and took the bags from my hands. I went back out to the car and got the other bags, brought them in.

"Did you hear me?"

"No," I said.

"I said you need a dick!"

"No, you need a dick. I need some drugs."

"Dwayne called while you were out. He's coming over. He's got a dick and drugs."

"I ran into your dad at the grocery store," I said.

"Really?"

"Yeah. I told him he should call or stop over and you know what he said?"

She stood there, looking small.

"He said you were no damn good, worse than your mother! Ha! Yeah, that's what he said! He said I should steal everything I could get and steal your mom's car and drive to California; get as far away from you two as I could, that you both would suck the life out of me if I didn't. That I would be one of those walking corpses, worse than a junkie, slobbering on myself in soup kitchens, shitting my pants and walking around all day and not even noticing."

She screamed: "OH, NO!" and burst into tears, ran upstairs to her room.

"Ha-ha! Yes! That's what he said," I yelled up the stairs. "He said I would be one of those people that shit themselves and dug it out of their pants! Played with it and painted shit paintings with it! That they would find me on the sidewalk with huge shit murals on the walls of buildings next to me and I would be blubbering nonsense about my great art! That they would take me away to the mental hospital and try to get it out of me, how I went crazy and I would hold out for a while, see? I would hold out and be honorable because I loved you but they would give me shock treatments and put things under my fingernails, do the Chinese water torture, starve me and I would give you up! Then they would come for you and take everything you have! It would be like this all over again but with supervision!"

I guessed that was enough and she knew who was boss. I made myself a sandwich, poured a glass of milk and took it out back to eat at the picnic table. It had turned out to be a nice day. The lawn looked good but I noticed some of the bushes needed trimming. I'd do that next week. I tried daydreaming about the band: We had made it big. The limo was taking us to Madison Square Garden. The concert was sold out. I sat in the back sipping something expensive in a brandy snifter and looking at all the mortals on the sidewalks. I was thinking, here we go… We've been playing the same songs over and over again all over the world. I tried to force the daydream into something positive but then it seemed false, contrived. I was grumpy about it. It was boring. That couldn't be the way it really was.

I finished eating and went back inside and washed the plate and glass. There wasn't a sound coming from upstairs. I had expected her to play the records I hated really loud but there was nothing. I looked at the clock and sat on the couch, picked up the remote and flipped through the channels. Nothing. I thought about heroin for a bit, no. I lit a cigarette and it tasted bad.

The doorbell rang and I went to the door. It was Dwayne. I let him in and he went upstairs, knocked on Cindy's door. "Hey. It's Dwayne." I heard the door open and heard it close. I sat there. The doorbell rang again, it was Tim, the lawyer. I handed him the bills to pay and he gave me $250.

"The yard looks nice," he said.

"Thank you," I said and slammed the door in his face.

Some music came down from upstairs, the radio. I didn't want to think about it; took my car, drove up to Lonnie's and played my guitar for a while. I was no poopie painter, I had plans! I had a sense of class! A new song started coming out. It was something mournful, a dirge-type thing. I poured my heart into it. It was almost there by the time I had to go get Nick at the train station.

20   The Harrisburg train station was downtown
in an area filled with decrepit buildings. Beat up bars and
hotels and rooming houses. Greasy spoon diners. I tried
to imagine it down there in the '40s and '50s before the
white flight. Real nightlife. Fedoras and skirts. Class. Even
in the '60s and early '70s, there was something there. I
remembered going to pick my dad up after work with
my mom and sister. We'd go to the Alva Restaurant by
the train station and then we'd walk around and look at
the Christmas window displays in the stores that would
eventually flee to the suburban malls. Dad would tell
stories and show us around; I was in awe of him.

The train was on time. Nick came out and I beeped the
horn. We got his bag in the trunk and got out of there.

"Well?" he said.

"Well what?"

"Did you think about it?"

"I can't right now," I told him.

"Ahh, that's cool. You got those women you're living
with right? Man! That must be great!"

"It's all right."

"I got a new girl up in the city."

"You love her?"

"What? Love her, ha! Man, you all right?"

We got there.

"It's great to be back with you guys," Nick said as he
plugged in to his amp. "This looks great. You guys have
it all set up."

Lonnie sat at his drums. I plugged in and we went
through a few songs. Monica gave us beers and Nick
broke out a bag of weed. We played for an hour or so; it
had been a while. It felt good.

We took a break and Nick told us of all his adven-
tures in the city, all about his job, how he got us the
gig. "You guys need to get up there with me, it's really
happening!"

Monica asked where Cindy was. I told her home and Monica said she would call her.

"No, I'll do it," I said, and picked up the phone. I dialed the number and watched Monica's pussy roll around. Nick and Lonnie had gone out back into the yard to talk and Monica was looking at me.

"Hello?" Cindy said.

"Hey Cindy," I said.

She hung up on me.

"You want to come party with us tonight? Oh, really? No, that's all right."

"Let me talk to her," Monica said.

"Cindy, Monica wants to talk to you. Oh? Okay, I'll tell her. All right, see you later." I hung up.

"She said she'd catch you later. She's got friends over," I told Monica.

"Damn, another night with the boys." She got up and looked out back. "Lonnie and Nick are out there," she said.

"Yep."

"What do you think of that?" she said pointing to the picture on the phone.

"It's nice. Got another beer?"

"You know where they are. Get one for me too."

I went out to the refrigerator and got them, came back in. She took hers and chugged it down, slammed the bottle on the coffee table. I looked out the window. Lonnie and Nick were out there under the stars, talking, smoking cigarettes. I heard Lonnie laughing.

Lonnie wrote some of our greatest songs, different than the stuff me and Nick wrote, really quite marvelous. I didn't know how it worked but there was something magical about the way we worked together, all bringing ideas and blending them into songs better than what any one of us could imagine alone. They were family, the family you chose and not the one you were born into. It

was better than that. Men do this, they push frontiers.
It might kill them but they push. It might...

"Tony?"

"Yes, Monica?"

"Go outside with your friends," she said.

Outside we talked and agreed to take the band to the
next level. New York City, here we come. Wooo. Nick had
brought some mushrooms and we each took a gram. We
went back inside and he gave Monica a gram. We drank
and smoked. The mushrooms kicked in and we played
for hours, just jamming, manic playing. Monica danced
like a go-go girl. This is overdrive: flashing lights, colors,
fingers running the frets, we build our own world like
this, see? We live in it and it's ours. We went to that place
where there was no language or maps.

Several hours later:

"You're not really like that."

I sat up in bed. "What time is it?" I asked Cindy.

She looked at the clock next to the bed and looked
at me. "Did you really run into my dad?"

"Yeah. He didn't say that stuff though."

"You really hurt me and then you just sounded crazy.
What the hell's wrong with you, man?"

"I can't live with people. I'm sorry."

"Well, it's not okay but I knew you were a bit bent
from the start."

"Where's Dwayne?"

"He went off. Said he has some new girlfriend. A
freakin' blonde!"

"I thought you would have stayed up all night with
him."

"That's what he thought too," she said. "You sure
came in late."

"Nick brought some mushrooms. We played for the
longest time. My fingers hurt. We must have jammed

for six hours."

"Well, get a shower. You stink. After that, if you're nice, I'll make you some lunch."

I got out of bed and Cindy stopped at the door. "I'm sorry too, about what I said. You've been through some bad stuff and I sometimes forget that."

"That's all right," I said.

"No it's not. Tony?"

"What?"

"You really scare me sometimes. You were screaming in your sleep this morning. I tried to wake you but couldn't. It really freaked me out."

She stood there for a bit, looking at me. I shrugged my shoulders and she went downstairs.

I sang in the shower: James Brown – *Try Me*, badly. The Animals – *A Girl Named Sandoz*, better. Syd Barrett – *No Good Trying*, that was it. I could hear the organ spilling out of the showerhead.

She had gone all-out with lunch, made spaghetti and a salad and garlic bread. I was hungry and ready.

"I want to show you something before I feed you," she said and walked to the back room.

I followed.

"I took you out of my painting last night," she explained.

I looked at it. How long had she been working on this thing?

"That's fine," I said. "Let's eat!"

"No, wait. That's not what I wanted to show you."

She pulled out a canvas that had been leaning face-first against the wall and held it up. It looked like a portrait of me but it didn't really look like me. This pseudo-me had vomit coming out of his mouth and bugs crawling out his ears. The eyes were all right though.

"What the hell is that?" I asked.

"It's the first painting I ever did spontaneously. It's

you. Well, the you I was mad at. Don't you see? I captured your ugliness, your rage!"

"I like it!" I said.

"I thought you would."

We had lunch out back at the picnic table and she was saying some things about Dwayne, how they did some coke and then he didn't want to fuck her, just wanted to hustle her into buying more coke.

"I told you he was a dick," I said and went to get another plateful. It was good. I didn't know she could cook. She was delighted with my hunger, told me to eat more! Yes!

"You've been good for me," she said, and then looked off into the tree line. A flock of birds were chattering in the trees. They'd fly around and then light again, they looked happy. The phone rang and she went to get it, came back out, said, "It's for you." I gulped down some more and took a few forkfuls of salad, then went to the phone.

It was Mick Angst. We had a gig that night at one of his hardcore shows.

"Tony! This is gonna be fantastic! You guys are bringing your PA, right?"

"I told you I would."

Yes, the show started at eight. Yes, we'd be there by 7:30 with the PA. I knew we wouldn't get paid. Knew he promised money to the out-of-town bands that he had booked but he still laid promises of $100 on me. Okay, okay. We'll be there.

"Who was that?" Cindy said.

"It was Mick Angst. You want to come to the show tonight?"

"Oh, yes. I am so gonna look like your slut tonight."

I ate some more and thought about it, smiled. "Thanks for the meal, Cindy. You're a fine cook."

She nodded and looked off again. The birds flew around. She was smiling. I didn't know how it worked or what to do but it seemed okay. We'd play along. See what happened.

Nick, who was staying up at Lonnie's place for the weekend, thought he could get his old pal Jeff to take our stuff over in his truck, but found out Jeff was back in Dauphin County Prison for assault and battery. We ended up getting all our gear in Lonnie's car, Lois's car which Cindy drove, and mine. Angst had rented out a VFW for the evening. It was an all-age show with five bands including us. The headliner was from Boston and several other bands were from the Maryland/Baltimore/DC area. We were the only local band and the place was packed with kids. We went on third, after one band that had a singer who sang with a fake English accent. It seemed to be the thing, the punk thing to do, in the early '80s. It was laughable. Nick got into a shouting match with the singer who was talking shit about us on the stage. When they left, Nick went after the guy and he ran. I walked out to see. Nothing. The guy was talking tough but wouldn't fight. There were some cinder blocks out there and I grabbed two and asked Nick to grab two.

"What for?" he asked.

"You'll see."

Lonnie just stood there, chuckling.

"What the hell's so funny?" I asked him.

"Nothing."

I put the blocks down. Nick stood there with the two in his hands.

"You guys think we'll get paid this time?" I asked.

"No," they replied in unison.

"Let's end it," I said.

After those guys were done clearing their stuff off the stage, we set up. I placed the cinder blocks in front of me, in front of the mike stand.

We took the stage and roared into our set. The kids moshed and the mosh circle came around me as I sang and played. It felt good. Midway through the set I announced that we had records available, to see the nice lady in the back if anyone wanted some. I pointed and people looked. Cindy stood up and waved. Then there was more roaring through songs, more moshing and mayhem.

Toward the end I held up a steel pipe while Nick and Lonnie played the intro to one of our songs. I looked over at Nick and looked at the blocks. He smiled. I looked out at Angst who was at the back of the hall. He got the idea and waved his hands like, no, no. I busted the blocks up into rubble. The kids loved it when you destroyed shit. The cinder rubble got tossed around and some kids got bloody in the pit. We did our last song and finished them off with pummeling feedback. Lonnie jumped up from behind his drums, grabbed two cymbals and placed them overturned on either side of me while Nick and I did our aural Armageddon act. He filled them with lighter fluid, lit them and ran back to his drums, did a Keith Moon routine, beating the hell out of them, kicking them over. I leaned over and turned my amp up to 10, took my SG and stuck the end of the neck in the floor. I bent the neck, played with the feedback. The flames on either side of me went up five feet.

Then some kids kicked over the cymbals and lit the stage on fire.

The lights went on and the power to the stage went off. There was some yelling and screaming. We quickly got our stuff packed in our cars and drove off...

Driving back I looked at Cindy in Lois's car following me and I thought of the great couples in rock. Sonny and Cher. James and Carly. John and Yoko. Sid and Nancy. The local TV news people were there interviewing us and I said, "No, we aren't punk rock. We create creases in time. We make wormholes."

"You've really taken the area by storm," the news lady said while the cameraman filmed us. "I've heard that you don't care for New Wave even though most people identify you with that."

"People need to label things in order to understand them, in order to have a place to put things in their minds," Lonnie said.

"We plow people. Think of us as meat grinders," Nick said.

"Oh, I see," the cute news lady said.

"No you don't," Lonnie said.

"Cut it!" she said. "Cut and wrap!"

21

The Appalachian Trail crosses over North Mountain at Longs Gap after meandering across the Cumberland Valley. It was Monday morning when I told Cindy that we were going for a hike if she was up to it. Lois had called Sunday afternoon while I was taking Nick back to the train station and had talked to her daughter for the longest time, saying she could only call Sundays and couldn't receive calls, that things were weird and she was suffering. Lois told Cindy she loved her, something she rarely said. The words were on the tip of Cindy's mouth but she could not speak them. "All right," Cindy had said. "So you'll call next Sunday?"

"Yes. I'll call," Lois had said.

"I miss you," was all Cindy could manage.

We drove west for eight miles and then turned up Longs Gap Road. The police never came knocking after the gig fire but I had received an angry phone call from Mick Angst filled with idle threats and garbage talk. I had pretended to listen but had actually put down the phone and made coffee. When I came back, he was still at it.

"So, they aren't pressing charges?" I asked.

"No. The lighter fluid burned off and didn't catch anything on fire. But the gig got shut down, man!"

"It was kinda cool," I said.

"No, it wasn't! I lost my ass with those people!"

"The kids loved it and we sold twenty records."

"Fuck you, Tony."

I hung up on him.

I pulled to a stop at the base of the mountain where the road ended and the trail began.

"So this is your special place?" Cindy asked.

"No, it's up there. You sure you want to do this? It's a long hike."

"Yeah, man. You ain't so tough. Anywhere you can go I can go."

"That's the spirit," I said.

We got out and started walking. The trail went sideways up the mountain but it was steep.

"How far is it?" she asked after a bit.

"It takes about an hour to get where we're going," I told her.

It was hot out and I had brought a jug of water. We stopped to take a drink and then walked on. A quarter of the way up there was a Jeep wrecked on its side. We looked at it and went on. The trail was filled with ruts and rocks.

"An old friend from high school showed me this place," I told her.

"Who?"

"Steve Logan. Last time I saw him he was really strung out. Fucker was all-state wrestling champ in the day though."

I didn't tell her the whole story, how his dad was rich, bought him a car and when he cracked the thing up, bought him another. That they gave him everything and he wound up worse off than me. He had heart though. He was a freakin' nut but we were friends. Were.

"Did you ever go up over Sterretts Gap?" I asked. "We used to go up there. There's a place to park at the top? You know, by the radio tower. You ever stop there?"

"No."

"Ha! We climbed that radio tower one night. Had to get over the barbed-wire fence first. It was in the dead of winter, cold as hell, wind howling. Anyhows, across the street from the radio tower is an old road. It's all broken up now; you could never get a car up there, but if you walk up there's a foundation for a building. The linoleum floor is still there; I think it was a diner or a bar. If you walk further up the mountain, you'll get to the crest. I once sat up there, again, in the winter, we were all stoned but it was daylight this time. To the north we watched a veil of snow coming toward us slowly and to the south, in the valley, it was sunny."

"So?"

"It was really something. I think philosophers would have called it sublime. I dunno about that but it was like we got there at just the right time to witness it."

"Look at the view!"

Cindy stopped. There was a break in the tree line and you could see out and down to the valley. We were both breathing hard and sweating. We looked.

"That's nothing," I told her. "Let's keep going."

We continued.

"Anyhows, up there at that place I was telling you about? It's loose rocks and boulders at the top. Weird, because most peaks are smooth from erosion or they have trees and dirt. But not up there. It's like a huge rock pile; nothing will grow up there. You know what I heard?"

She didn't say anything, just kept walking along beside me.

"Cindy?"

"I'm listening."

"I heard that the ice shelf from the ice age deposited those rocks up there. That this was as far south as the ice got before retreating back north. Can you imagine that?"

"Must have been a big damn glacier."

"No doubt. You think that's why the Cumberland Valley is so wide compared to the other valleys? From the runoff? That's what I think."

"You're the coolest geek I ever met, Tony."

"Ha! Thanks."

"Where do you come up with this shit?"

"I used to read a lot." An understatement. I devoured libraries when I was a kid.

Half an hour later, we reached the summit. The trail bent north and over the top, then went down into Perry

County. I stopped in a patch of trees and said, "Here we are."

"This is it?"

"No. Follow me," I said, and led her down a little footpath between the trees. "Watch your step."

She put her hand on my back. We came out of the trees and walked onto the white cliffs that overlooked the valley below.

"This is it," I told her.

On a clear day you could see twenty miles in either direction; you could see til the earth curved away. It was a clear day. She just stared.

"It's really something, isn't it?"

"It's beautiful," she said.

We sat next to each other and looked at it while we passed the water jug. A hawk was soaring a mile out, riding the hot air currents. She pointed and I nodded my head. She looked at me; looked into my eyes and looped her arm around mine. There was something there. She smiled and shook her hair, looked back out. The hawk eventually made its way overhead. It did a short circle over us and then went on to the east, riding the ridge currents. The world lay at our feet.

We did not speak until hours later when we were halfway back down the mountain and even then, it was hesitantly, in hushed tones.

22   Something had happened on North Mountain that day but we never spoke of it and never went back. Cindy covered over the masterpiece she had been working on forever with mad swirls of paint. I asked her what she was doing and she said, "It needs to be thick, really thick. Then I'll put something on top of it."

"Ha! Yes! That's the ticket!" I told her.

I continued my sissy stage and moved into the guest room. We treated each other kindly, like we loved each other, but we didn't sleep together. I had gotten us a big bag of pot and we smoked constantly. She stayed in the room with her paints and I set up my amp and stuff in the guest room, started making home recordings, bouncing tracks between cassette decks. Days went by like this, coffee and weed and at the end of the days we would see and hear what each other had done. Cindy filled all the empty canvases she had with paint. There we were on the mountain, there was one with the hawk (looking like a winged demon), there was her mom and dad, all surreal and melting. I did a whole cassette album of songs, some old ones I had and some new. I did percussion tracks with pots and pans and boxes, did guitar tracks, vocal tracks and vocal harmony tracks. I did kazoo tracks and imagined saxophones.

Nights were for the party scene. It seemed we were the hot couple everyone wanted at their parties. There was drinking and madness but we stayed away from the hard drugs that were all around. It was something unspoken, we just watched out for each other. There was a cocaine epidemic going on at the time, it was everywhere. Did you ever see someone so strung out on cocaine that they looked like they took a dry shotgun blast to the face?

Driving home one night I sideswiped a row of parked cars in my Mustang. We actually got stuck to the last one in the row and had come to a dead stop.

"He-he," Cindy said. "Did you mean to do that?"

"I'm drunk. You wanna drive?"

"No. I'm all fucked up."

"You didn't get into a tequila drinking match with a coke freak."

"I told you so," she said in a singsong voice.

"Who won?"

"My hero. Now, could you please get us home somehow?"

I hung my head out of the window. It was late or early. There were stars overhead; there were houses all dark and there was no one else on the road.

"Where the fuck are we?" I asked.

"New Cumberland. Somewhere in New Cumberland."

I got out of the car and stumbled around a bit. I fell down in the middle of the street and howled the drunk howl.

"Goddamnit, Tony! Get back in the car and get us the hell out of here!" Cindy yelled.

I knew her door was pinned against the parked car. I lay there in the middle of the street. I felt sleepy... The dream was about the band, it was another interview: I was spouting politics and metaphysics while Nick and Lonnie shook up beer cans and sprayed them around.

"Goddamnit, Tony!" It was Cindy. She was picking me up. Must have crawled over to get out my side.

"Somebody call a cop!" I yelled.

"Get the fuck up and get us out of here!"

"All right, get back in the car; I'll take care of everything. Tony'll take care of it."

She dropped me and got back in. I found I couldn't really walk so I crawled back to the car, got in and backed up. The sound of crunching metal. The passenger door handle ripped back across the car we were pinned against. I swung the wheel and the front bumper of my car ripped the back bumper off the car we were pinned against. It fell to the street.

"Ha-ha! I win," I said and stopped. We seemed to still be moving. I thought maybe if I would vomit it would clear my head.

"You're a fucking nut," she said.

"Don't say that."

"You are, you know. You're really crazy."

"Oh no, that's not crazy. I could show you crazy."

"Oh yes, show me. Be a big man."

I slammed the gas and spun the wheel, forgetting I was still in reverse. We hit something and came to a stop. It might have been another car, I didn't know, didn't look. I slammed it in drive and stomped it again and shot across the street, hitting the car I was pinned against before. Cindy grabbed the dashboard and I saw fear in her eyes. Good. Some lights came on in some houses. I started feeling bad about it and drove off.

We got home somehow and Cindy got out of the car and walked up to the house. I sat there. Everything was spinning. I was on a merry-go-round being interviewed by Circus Magazine.

Do you dye your hair?

No.

Let's talk about the music.

You talk about it.

"Tony?"

"What?"

"Are you going to come in?"

"Eventually. Ta kill ya. Er, ta kill ya," I said. I wanted to laugh or howl but it wasn't there.

Cindy opened my door.

"Man, the other side of your car is all fucked up."

"We had fun."

"You had fun."

"Back up."

"What?"

I vomited on the driveway and she jumped back.

"Eww," she said.

I got out and slipped on it, landed in it, cracked my head against the driveway. Everything went black.

Then somebody was shaking me. I didn't like it, wanted to sleep. A man needs his sleep. They kept shaking me, they needed a good ass kicking. I'll tell ya, one more shake and I'll…

They were saying something. There was another shake. I sat up.

"Goddamnit!" I said.

It was Sal from next door. I had talked to him from time to time while working outside, he seemed like a good guy.

"Oh, Sal," I said, looking around.

He laughed. "Man. I tied a few on in my college days too," he said. "You get inside and get yourself cleaned up and I'll help you with your car."

I stood up. My legs were back. "Beer and ta kill ya."

"Tequila?"

"Never again, Sal."

"Get your ass inside and get out of those clothes, boy!"

I went in and stripped. There was dried vomit on my pants and shirt. I had a bump on the back of my head, it felt crusty. I threw my clothes down the basement stairs and made coffee. Upstairs, Cindy was still asleep. Hello, Cindy. Shower and teeth brushing and water drinking. Walk a mile in my shoes, Circus Magazine. Walk a mile in my shoes all you know-it-alls. We'll see. Oh, yes…

"Cindy, I love you."

She woke up.

"Oh, I tried to pick you up and bring you inside but I couldn't. You were bleeding. I thought you broke your skull and was gonna call an ambulance but I was too fucked up."

"I made coffee," I said.

"You're all right?"

"God watches over the crippled and crazy."

"You think?"

"No. Look. I'm going out to hang with Sal. There's coffee."

"I'm going back to sleep for a while, Tony."

"All right," I said and walked out.

"Tony?"

"Yes?"

"I'm glad you're all right and I don't really think you're crazy."

"That makes one of us," I said and again, started walking away.

"Tony?"

"Yes?"

"I love you."

Outside, Sal had finished washing the vomit off the driveway and was standing there smoking. I had my cup of coffee and asked him if he wanted a cup.

"Fuck that. I had my morning coffee hours ago. You know what time it is?"

"It's eleven," I said, taking a guess.

"Well, that's a start," Sal said, looking at his watch. "It's noon. Man. Your car is all fucked up. Did you see the passenger side?"

I walked around to look at it. There were several different colors of paint scraped down the side. There was a big gouge where the door was dented in. I walked around the whole thing. The front and rear bumper were also dented with paint.

"What happened?" Sal asked. "It looks like you were in a demolition derby!"

"I don't remember, I was drunk," I said. A flat-out lie.

I always remembered everything.

"Well, like I said, I been there. We're gonna have to get the paint off your car. It's evidence."

"You been there?"

"Oh, yes. I could tell you tales," he said, and then did as we scrubbed the paint off. His college days in Syracuse. Hot rods and pussy, man! "All the chicks dug us motorheads. You a motorhead?"

"I used to be. I'm playing with a rock band now though, for the summer."

"Ah, man! That's cool! I always wished I could play an instrument. What do you play?"

"Guitar. I sing too. I'm the guitarist and singer in this local band."

"Uh-huh," Sal said.

After we got the paint cleaned off the car he said he was going back home.

"Thanks for the help, Sal," I said. "You aren't working today?"

"Ah, I manage this food distribution plant. I come and go as I please."

"That sounds cool."

He looked at me. "It's boring. And you're full of shit. I don't believe you're Lois's nephew and don't believe you're a singer. I don't know what's up with you man, but I still like you. You really going to Penn State?"

"Yes. And I really do sing with a band."

"You ain't Lois's nephew though, are you?"

"No."

"Where's your family?"

"We don't get along."

He looked at me, hard-like. "Where's Cindy?"

"She's upstairs, sleeping. Sal?"

"Yeah?"

"Don't worry none about that. I would protect Cindy with my life."

He looked at me and pulled out a cig, lit it, offered me one.

"No thanks," I said.

"Kathy said she was going to make lunch. I told her to hold it, that I was gonna come out to pick your sorry ass up off the driveway. She said, no, don't go over there. The Williamses are beasts and that guy that lives there seems like real trouble. I thought, fuck it. The neighborhood is boring, all our kids are off in college and I feel half dead already. I thought, here's this guy, lying on the pavement that looks like somebody I used to know when I was younger. I hated you for that. You can only really hate something you really know; something you hate in yourself," he said and then looked off as if he had gone into a reverie.

"Fuck," he said.

"What?"

"Korea. You remind me of this guy I knew in Korea."

"You were friends?"

"Best friends. You wouldn't believe the battles we went through," he said and looked off again.

I looked where he was looking. Sky. Clouds. Sun. The sun was a problem.

"He didn't make it?"

"No," Sal said.

He looked lost, old. I thanked him again and started back inside.

"Tony?"

"Yeah?"

"Stop over any time. Stop over tonight if you like. I've got beer. We can shoot the shit."

"I'll do that," I told him and he walked back to his house. Yeah, right. I'm gonna hang with an old man and listen to his stories. Like I cared. I was Tony Diggs, the soon-to-be famous rock god. Women fell to my feet and millions of dollars were just out there, waiting for me to grab them. I would assassinate these suburbs and all the people in them. I would brutalize them and throw the farce of America back in its face in song.

Circus Magazine: Tell us about the time you lived in the suburbs.

Me: Well, I was living in this place I called the dollhouse.

Circus Magazine: Oh, yes. The place you sang about in *Fucked and Furious*, your first album.

Me: Yes, heh-heh, they thought I was a mere mortal.

Circus Magazine: Is it true that the neighbors were all Satan worshippers?

Me: Ah, yeah. The goat sacrifices and the three-eyed lady...

After dinner that evening, Cindy went off to Stacy's for a girl's night out. I fucked around in my little studio for a bit, recording some guitar track, but my heart wasn't in it. I called a few people on the phone and talked, then got off the phone. Sandman had some morphine. Lonnie was just chilling. Come on over. No, just calling. I'll see ya later. All right. Right. I'll make the scene in some bars later, I told myself. Yeah, that's what I'd do. I'd put on my white bucks and black leather pants and make the scene. There's no real scene. You hate everybody. Oh. Right.

I smoked a little weed and then went downstairs to get a glass of milk. Then I walked over to Sal's place and rang the doorbell.

23 Dreams of flying again. Arms out, machine guns in arms and shitting bombs. It was war, you used what you had. But it wasn't that great, I got shot down, spun in and just before I hit, I woke. That's not right, I thought, the woman you love is sleeping in the next room and here you are. She finally said *I love you*, and here you are. You're not right; you should be with her and quit pretending to have such high moral standards. I know what's wrong, you're bored. No, she's not boring, you are. You fuck. Get the band moving, get some momentum going with the band or just shut up and get a straight job. Do something, you fuck!

We have a gig coming up soon in the city!

It's gonna be for shit! Nobody will be there and the ones that do come will laugh!

I didn't want to get out of bed; just wanted to lay there. Sal and I had drank beer and talked for hours on his back porch. He was way cooler than I thought he would be, guy had great war stories, all kinds of stories, had really lived. I had to make some shit up about my family and Penn State, it sounded good when I said it, it was believable but, in the morning, I didn't feel so good about it. The weird thing of it was: I had told him a truth I had never told anyone. And I mean, no one. It was something I barely knew myself. It was during a lull in the conversation when Karen had gone in to get herself a soda and bring us some more beer.

"She's decided she likes you," Sal said.

"You think? She doesn't say much."

"Yeah, I think. If she didn't she wouldn't even hang out with us. She wouldn't run for beer. Just wait, she'll bring out a plate of crackers and cheese. She might even offer to cook something."

We sat there, sipping beer.

"I'm gonna be a writer some day, Sal," I said.

"Oh really? What will you write about?"

"I dunno. Life. I haven't really lived enough to do it yet but think someday I might have something."

Sal didn't say anything, lit a cigarette and blew out a cloud. There were fireflies in the backyard, flitting about, and there was a crescent moon overhead. Off in the distance, there was the sound of workers, working on the highway that was across the creek and over the hill. They were widening it to three lanes in either direction and worked 24/7. Jackhammers.

Karen brought out beer, crackers and cheese and said, "If you boys are going to talk and drink all night, I'm going to have to feed you."

"Tony?" Sal asked. "We gonna talk and drink all night?"

"If you're up to it, I am."

"Karen? You hear that? We have company for the night."

"It's Friday night!" Karen said.

"Friday!" Sal said.

"Friday! Drink with us, Karen!" I said.

"Let's start the grill," Karen said and went back into the house.

"She doesn't drink anymore, Tony," Sal said.

"Oh. I'm sorry."

"That's all right. She's a good woman."

"I never doubted it."

"She's making us hamburgers now," he said.

"All right."

"I'll start the grill," he said and went to it, pouring charcoal briquettes on the grill and pouring fluid, lighting it. I wasn't that hungry but went along with it.

"Can I use your bathroom?"

"It's down the hall to the right."

I found it, took a piss and out of habit, looked in the medicine cabinet. The usual suspects: high blood pressure meds for the man and Valium for the woman. The communal antacid and aspirin and other things. Nothing good though; I don't know why I looked. Walking back out, I paused at the kitchen to look at Karen. She smiled at me over her shoulder.

"I make great burgers," she said. "You'll see."

Outside, Sal was standing up and looking off to the north.

"You hear it?" he said.

"Yeah."

"Progress, right?"

"Fuckin' hell," I said.

We drank our beers and Sal went in to get us two more.

"You hungry?" he asked when he got back.

"Not really."

"Me neither. Could you do me a favor though?"

"What's that?"

"Eat. Act hungry. She's a good woman."

"All right."

"Tony?"

"Yeah?"

"If you ever do become a writer, do it right, okay?"

"All right," I said.

We drank and talked 'til late. I met Cindy at a gig. No, she's not really my girlfriend, just a friend. How's that work? It doesn't even sound right, does it? No. Ha-ha, fuck. Yes, Lois is in Italy now. I think she's going off to Germany next...

I got out of bed and went to take a piss. It was a long, boring one. I stood there. My woman was in the other room, I heard her, she was sleeping. No, that's not right, she was awake and waiting for her man to come in to be with her. That's right.

I went downstairs and smelled coffee.

"Hello," someone said to me in the kitchen.

"Hello."

"You're Tony, right?"

I looked at her. A petite blonde, around twenty, wearing one of my thrift-shop dress shirts.

"Where'd you get the shirt?" I asked.

"Cindy gave it to me. Isn't it pretty?"

"It looks good on you," I said.

"Do you want some coffee? I made coffee."

"Yeah, I could dig some coffee."

"What do you like in it?"

"Milk."

"No sugar?"

"No, just milk."

She poured me a cup and bent over to get the milk from the fridge. Oh, yes. Look. Will you look at that? Uh-huh, fuck. I see. She's pouring milk in my coffee. She's handing it to me. I'm saying something. No, I'm not, I'm just standing there in my underwear.

"My name's Toni too, but with an I," she said.

"That's nice," I said and took the coffee to the table. Sat down.

"He-he," she said.

"What?"

"You know you have a big hole in the back of your underpants?"

"I like it like that."

She stood there looking at me. She had perky little tits.

She poured two cups of coffee. She put sugar in both and then put a little milk in both. Then she took the milk and bent over again to put it back in the fridge. She pretended to look around in there for a bit.

"You know when you bend over, I can see your pussy?"

She looked at me over her shoulder. "He-he," she said.

"It looks smooth."

"I'm shaving Cindy later," she said. "Wanna watch?"

"I can't," I said.

"Oh, yes. That's what I heard."

She took the two coffees upstairs.

The phone rang and I picked it up. It was Nick.

"Hey, I'm up at Lonnie's. You coming up soon?"

"What time is it?" I asked and then looked at the kitchen clock.

"It's almost noon. And it's Saturday. What are you doing?"

"I just woke up," I said.

More talk. Okay, right. I'll be up.

I went upstairs to shower and dress. There was music playing softly in Cindy's room, the radio, and I smelled marijuana. After I dressed I knocked lightly on her door.

"Cindy?"

"What?" I heard.

"I'm leaving for a while," I said to the door.

She said to come on in, honey. I did. They were in bed together.

"Did you meet Toni?"

"Uh-huh."

Toni giggled again. A blonde giggler. Go on, say something pimp-like. Go on.

"I'll be at Lonnie's all day and probably most of the night."

"All right. See ya."

"See ya, Tony," Toni said.

Lonnie's sister was outside washing her car when I pulled up. She said hi.

"What happened to your car?" she asked.

"Oh, nothing."

"Yeah, right."

"It's fine; I like it like that. People get out of your way."

"Uh-huh. They're downstairs."

I went down.

24

Thursday afternoon I was in Lonnie's station wagon on our way to NYC. We had all our gear in the back. It fit, but barely. The girlfriends were told that if they wanted to come, they'd have to drive in a separate car. They declined.

"Monica's been on my ass about getting a job," Lonnie said.

"That bitch!"

"Yeah, right? I give her a place to stay and then this."

"So?"

"What?"

"You're thinking about it?"

"I can't work, man. Once you start that, you're done."

We rolled up 78. Lonnie lit another cig. He smoked cigarettes constantly but was one of the few people I knew that didn't smoke pot. I thought that was cool.

"I gotta do something, man," I said. "Lois is gonna be back from rehab soon and I don't think I can deal with the psychodrama."

"You fuck her and her daughter? How's that work?"

"Well, it's odd. You'd think it would be really cool and it was for a while. But it gets old. Confusing. I didn't tell you that she's paying me to stay there?"

"What?"

"Oh, yeah. Don't tell anybody, I feel a little funny about it. Hundred bucks a week. And she pays for food on top of all the house bills. Hundred bucks a week, free and clear. Her lawyer comes once a week and gives me the cash."

Lonnie looked at me and then looked back at the road.

"Go on," I said.

"What? I didn't say anything."

"Say, 'You're a gigolo, Tony.'"

"I didn't say that."

"You wouldn't," I said.

"What's that supposed to mean?"

"Never mind."

"Goddamnit, Tony."

"Don't get mad."

We drove on in silence for a while. I tried to get something on the radio but there was nothing.

"So," Lonnie said, "what's Monica been doing at your place?"

"She hangs out with Cindy and Cindy's new friend, Toni. They smoke pot and listen to records," I lied.

"You ain't fucking her, are you?"

"Hell no. When they get together it's girl's night; I stay out of it."

"Girl talk?"

"Fuck. And how. I hide in my room. You know what I say. Let them get it out of their system so's we don't have to hear it."

What kind of ass turns down sex with two women one night and three the next? A pimp, that's what kind.

"What?" Lonnie said.

"I didn't say anything."

We drove on. Lonnie smoked and I looked out the window. The Holland Tunnel came and we went through it. Manhattan. All of a sudden it felt like we were in some movie. I was all wired up.

"Give me a smoke," I said.

"Since when do you smoke?"

"I smoke."

"No you don't. You quit, remember?"

"I want to quit again," I said.

He gave me one. It tasted good. We found the place in Chelsea and parked.

The place we were playing in was uptown on 38th St. by

8th Ave. The Hive. We were third on the bill and took the stage at eleven. There weren't too many people there. We blew through our set, there was some applause. I talked to the audience but they seemed listless, non-receptive. Where was the life, where was all the big-city life? It was somewhere, but not there. Fuck them. There was a courtyard out back and we took beers out there after. The friends that lived in the city and had come to see us had left. The next band started. They were horrible New Wave schlock. We didn't get paid but the barmaid gave us beer.

We sat at a table in the courtyard, not saying much. The barmaid came back out after a bit.

"You guys were really great!" she said. "I never heard anything like it."

We thanked her.

"No, I really mean it. You wouldn't believe the garbage I hear here, night after night."

"Like the shit they're playing now?" I asked.

"Oh, god. Those guys were here before. Long Island yuppies playing rock star in the city. They drag their boring friends and family along and brag about their draw. You wouldn't believe how many bands we get like that. Look, I can get you guys some more free beer if you like."

"You won't get into trouble?"

"Hell, I don't care. The old owner was way cooler. This new guy is a moron."

She took our orders and went back in. Nick lit a joint and passed it to me. She brought the beer out and leaned on my shoulder, handing them out. I told her she smelled nice and handed her the joint. She took a quick hit and handed it back.

"Damn. I'd like to stay out here but, work." She let go of my shoulder and walked back inside.

"Ha-ha!" Nick said. "You smell nice. What the hell

was that?"

"She did!"

"Man, Tony. Girl leans on you, breathes down your neck and, 'You smell nice?' Ha-haw!"

"Where's your woman, Nick?"

"Ah, hell. I couldn't fuck that anymore," he said. "Guess you're almost married now anyway. What's her name? Cindy? She's pretty hot."

A couple of long-haired guys came outside. They looked older.

"New Left! That's a cool name," one of them said.

"We dug your songs," the other said.

"Thanks, guys. Have a seat," Nick said.

They pulled up chairs and we bullshitted for a while. When the barmaid came back out and put her hand on my shoulder again, they insisted on buying us beers. I picked the half-joint up out of the ashtray and handed it to her, gave her a light. She took a good hit and went back in. I handed the joint to Nick and he took a hit, handed it back to me. The long-haired guys looked at me. I took the last hit and ashed it out.

They went on about this and that and I wasn't really listening, was in some odd headspace, some dead air where words didn't mean much. Nick was engaging them in conversation and Lonnie was adding this and that. I imagined being in a bubble and floating up, but not too far off the ground. I didn't want to look too far, see too much, no.

The girl came back out, handed beers around and whispered something in my ear. I reached up and she put something in my hand. I didn't look at her, just put it in my pocket. We were in my bubble.

A while later the long-hairs got up to leave.

"Hey!" I said to them.

They turned around.

"Tip the barmaid before you leave?"

They nodded and left.

We got our stuff packed away in Lonnie's car and he drove off back to PA. Nick and I walked over to 5th Ave to hail a cab.

"This is gonna be cool," Nick said.

"We'll see. Those guys seemed like real dimwits."

"Playing the 5th Avenue Pot Parade? Man! It's gonna be great!"

"If they're Yippies, then I guess the Yippies don't have much steam anymore."

"What the hell are you talking about?"

"Man, you don't know. I grew up on that shit. You ever read Abbie Hoffman's *Revolution for the Hell of It*? I read that book when I was in junior high. Freakin' David Peel? Man. Same thing. Me and my friends read and listened to that stuff before we even smoked pot! Those guys were a gas! But 'm not sure it swings right now. Back then it was new and real. It was Vietnam and Nixon and all that shit. Now, all they seem to care about is legalizing pot. What a bunch of fuckheads."

"I care about legalizing pot," Nick said, weakly.

"Sure you do. What you gonna do for a job then? What are all those so-called Yippies gonna protest then?"

We got a cab and went downtown. The so-called movement got high and lost their balls. They got high. Everybody got high. I hated them. I would assassinate them in songs and books... The cab dropped us off at St. Mark's Place. We went into St. Mark's Bar and Grill and looked. Choo-Choo wasn't there. We walked east to the International B&G. "Choo's probably down there," Nick said. Morrison was in my head – Summer's almost gone. Where will we be?

"Nick!" Choo said and stood up. "And Tony! Long time no see, Tony!"

We shook hands. There were some other people there that seemed glad to see me and Nick. Choo bought us beers and introduced me to people. There were handshakes and smiles, it seemed all right.

"I like these people," I told Nick after a while.

"I knew you would. It's good here, I told you."

"Yeah, it's good."

"What are you two talking about?" Choo-Choo asked and then went off to the jukebox and then called out, "Mary! Nick's friend is here from PA! "

Some old woman came out from the back of the bar somewhere. I looked at Nick. He nodded and smiled. "Mary," he said. I thought I was in some time warp. The bar was old, everything about it was old. There was an old-time tin ceiling, old, dark wood bar, half-decayed buck head on the wall, shit piled up in the back where they could have put a few pool tables.

Mary came out of the mess in the back, like she just woke up. She looked to be around eighty years old.

"Oh, Tony?" she said. "Nick told me so much about you, you are his good friend."

"Yes, I am," I said. "We are like brothers."

"I buy you drink. You stay, right? You stay and drink?"

"I stay," I said. "Nice to meet you, Mary."

"Oh, this is special night. Cathy," she said to the barmaid, "you give Tony and Nick drinks on me!"

I had no idea. Nick was so right about all these people. We had a fine time, drank entirely too much and, when last call came at four, Mary shooed everyone out but us and we closed the gates outside for her and had a few more drinks.

We stumbled back to Choo's place on E 3rd after five. I slept on the floor.

Sometime around noon, the phones started ringing. There were three of them lined up on the desk. Choo-Choo started answering. Nick took his bike and pack and hit the street. I pulled the phone number from my pocket and dialed.

"Amy? It's Tony. Uh-huh. Yes. No, here's no good. All right."

I scribbled the address down. "All right. Give me an hour or so."

Choo and I got off the phones at the same time. He looked at me and said, "I gotta take a shit. If the phone rings, could you answer it? Just tell 'em to hold."

"All right."

Don, another messenger, came out of the back bedroom. I sat down, picked one of the phones up, dialed.

"Cindy? Yeah, hi. It went all right. No. No. We got another gig out of it though. Yeah, next month. Why would you miss me? Uh-huh, right. I know. Yes. You all right? Oh, no. Don't do that. Really, just kick them out. Yes you can. Aw, hell, yes you can. Fuck. I want to stay a few days. Okay, I'll try and make it back tomorrow." The other phone started ringing. "Hey look. I gotta go. All right. Yes, me too."

I picked up the other phone and told them to hold.

Choo came out of the bathroom and said, "Whew!"

I told him there was someone waiting, handed him the phone and got out of his chair.

"Hey, Don? Where's 1 West 72nd St.?"

"Man, that's the Dakota. Right there on the corner of Central Park West and 72nd. Why?"

"I'm going up there," I said.

25 It was good to get outside.

No, sleeping on a floor didn't matter, it was fine. You just had to be drunk or crazy or tired or all three. Look, the little crowd of Ricans wants to mess with you. Think they hang out in front of the bodega all day?

I went into the bodega and got coffee. The one guy had a piece of wire, like he was gonna strangle me. Funny, they just want to see if they can get you all scared. The good old boys played games down home too. Fuckers. I could show them something but had a date. No, I didn't look at your women. No, I won't, you can have them. Yeah, we'll see. Ha-ha. You okay, blondie. All right, see ya's. See ya's around.

I walked over to Ave B and up. I was disorientated, didn't know my way around. There were people in the street, people hanging out windows yelling at people in the street. If you look sideways at them, they'll try and rip your white-boy guts out. All ya need is the walk, that's all. You get the walk and they smile. You don't even have to act cool, just get the walk and the third-eye stare. That's it. Hello. Nice day. Oh, yes. Really quite nice. Hiya. Look at this goofy-assed motherfucker strolling down the lane. Red hair pouring out of his head. Fucker looks lost, no, he's smiling. What the hell's wrong with this bastard? Heyya. M-huh. Heyya, kid.

I walked past Tompkins Square Park and up to Ave A. There were white people up there. I nodded at a few and said hello and they ignored me. That's how it goes. Elitism is the first cousin of barbarism. I know you fuckers from high school. Now you're all sleek and in another uniform but I still see ya's. You can turn your third eye off now, it ain't needed. Ain't gonna be nothing but art and its first cousin, politics here. Yeah, I see ya's. Fuckers.

I walked into the International Bar and Grill and had a seat at a table.

"Who da hell are you? Why don't you get a dahell out

of here?" Mary said after appearing from the back.

"Mary? I met you last night, remember? With Choo-Choo and Nick?"

She looked at me, blinked. "You help me close gates?"

"Yeah. I just wanted to sit here and drink my coffee, if that's okay."

"You no buy drink?"

"Nah. Maybe later."

"I buy you drink. You drink with old lady?"

"I shouldn't. You get drink and sit with me. I drink coffee. We talk."

She came back with drinks insisting I drink with her. "It's liquor, I think you like. Go good with coffee. Nostrovia," she said and sipped.

"Nostrovia," I said and drank it down. "Whew! That's good. What was that?"

She told me some name I couldn't pronounce, said it was from her country. What's that? Ukraine. The bastards drove us out. Some didn't make it. I made it out. May they burn in hell.

"You Choo-Choo's friend, right?"

"Yeah. I'm Choo-Choo's friend and Nick's friend."

"You move up here, they are good friends to have."

"Nick told you?"

"Yes, Nicky and Choo," she said.

We talked for a while, yeah, my grandpa came from Ireland. Drove out also. Yeah, may they burn in hell. "I gotta get some food," I said.

"Go to Stanley's. Is just up the block."

See ya later. See ya. You come back? Yeah, I come back, Mary. Uh-huh. Go eat.

Stanley's: up the block on Ave A. Dinky little place, like a bar but a diner. Barstool seats. Eggs, homefries, toast and coffee. Okay, sausage too. Uh-huh. Mary told me to come here. Uh-huh, yeah, from the International. "She came from the village that was a few miles from mine," Stanley said, "You know her?"

"I just met her. My friends know her." I'm just up visiting, etc.

"We feed you good here, right?" he said to his wife that was cooking.

"That's right, Stanley. Us Ukrainians just one big happy family."

"Don't listen to her," Stanley said, "she's grumpy today."

"I heard that! I'll beat you with a pan!"

"You do that, you won't get no lovin' tonight!"

"Don't be such a beast in front of the customers."

"I was just playing…"

It was good to see. Old folks that had been together for years. The food was good and cheap and the regulars just sat there not saying much. They had heard it before. I tipped them a buck and he looked at it like he never got tipped. Yeah, I'll be back. Some year. You kids play nice. Kids? You hear that, honey? He called us kids. "I'll hit him in the ass with this pan if he don't scoot."

Ha-ha. Lala. La-ti-da. Up on First Ave I looked for cabs. What was it? Lights on and they're taken? Something. I put up my hand and one pulled over. I got in and gave him the address.

"The Dakota?" he asked.

We went off. "What's the big deal about the Dakota?"

He looked at me in his mirror. "The Dakota is old, man."

"Fuck it. You care if I smoke?"

"You can smoke."

I didn't have any cigarettes.

"Got its name from the fact that, when it was built in 1884, it was so far uptown and away from all the fashionable residential areas, it might as well be in the

Dakota territories."

"Got a cigarette?"

"I don't smoke," he said and then went on. The walls were twenty-eight inches thick, they filmed Rosemary's Baby there. John and Yoko. That's right. That's where I heard of it. Strawberry Fields is across the street? Yep, in Central Park.

"You from out of town?"

"Yeah," I said. "My dog told me to go there and kill somebody."

"You're joking, right?"

"Yeah, little joke. I'm a funny person."

"I didn't think it was funny," he said and continued on with his historical overview of the Dakota.

I looked out the window. We were in some movie. I was taking a briefcase filled with pages from the novel I had slaved over for months to some famous editor. No, that's not right, I was going to meet some record producer that was a famous recluse and but suddenly became interested in producing again after hearing our tape. He called me all the time at the dollhouse. That's right. After a while, I quit answering the phone, told Cindy to tell him I was in my studio. Yeah, that's it. I was a freakin' genius and...

"Goddamnit, man! You should teach," I said.

That shut him up. We drove on.

"Columbia," he said.

"What?"

"I used to teach at Columbia."

"Columbia?"

"Yeah, uptown. Fuck Columbia."

We got there. Fuck Columbia. May they burn in hell.

I paid no mind to the huge archway entrance and went in, gave the concierge my name and told him, Adams.

He picked up the house phone and dialed.

Gothic, ain't it? Yup. Look at this guy. Phone dialin', uniform wearin'. Didn't call me sir til after he got off the phone, uh-huh. Go on up. There. The elevator is there, sir. Uh-huh, all right. Can't I wander around the court-yard a bit? Forget it. Go on up. All right.

The elevator guy looked straight ahead. We got up-stairs. Do I tip him? Look at me, fucker! Nope, there she is. He's lookin' at the young lady. Uh-huh, he's all right, it's all right. Thanks, Jimmy. Look at me Jimmy. Nope. Jimmy's gone. What's with Jimmy?

"Hiya, Amy," I said.

It was like that. Third eye blinkin' and then in my bubble. Fuck the world, let them burn in hell. Hello, hiya. Blinkblink.

"Hey, Tony. Come on in."

I followed her ass in, she was saying something. I stood there for a bit in the middle of her living room.

"Nice place," I said. Lame. Totally lame. Was a ge-nius in the cab though. It might come back, I might get something back.

"It's my parents' place," she said. "Would you like something to drink? We have soda, beer..."

"Stop," I said.

"What?"

"Come here," I told her.

"No, I don't think so. You come here."

I did. It's all right. Sometimes you have to give a little.

A while later, we were laying in her bed and I told her, "Someday, I'm gonna save you from this place."

She laughed. See? I am a funny man. What the hell do ex-Columbia teachers that drive cabs know? I rolled over and spooned her. She grabbed my hands in front of her and purred. Yes, purr kitten. Gargoyles flew around the building.

"I must show you around!" she suddenly exclaimed and jumped out of bed.

I looked at her body. I didn't deserve her, it was stupid. All my clever words were gone. Maybe she didn't care.

"Get dressed," she said as she threw on some clothes.

I did and she showed me around the place. Her mother and father did this and that. They won't be home til five, relax. You're so tense. It's all right, Tony, I like you. John and Yoko.

"Oh, yes. Yoko still lives upstairs," she said. "Charles Henri Ford lives next door, man!"

"Were you here when John Lennon got murdered?"

"Oh, yes. It was so sad. He was such a nice man but he seemed sad all the time anyway. Look at all my father's books, man!" She pulled me into another room.

I looked. It was a huge room with bookcases built into the walls. They were all filled.

"This is my dad's library," she said. "He's a publisher and knows all these famous people! You read?"

"I have read a lot," I told her.

"I thought you did, you can hear it in your songs. Look," she said.

I didn't know where to start. Picked up this and that book off the shelf, put them back.

"I've got to go back to PA tomorrow," I told her.

"Oh, no. We just met."

"I have to. Made a promise."

"Well, you want to meet Charles Henri Ford?"

"All right," I said.

We went next door and she knocked. An old man came to the door and said, "Well, hello, Amy," and let us in. We had tea with him and she told him I was a musician. He groaned.

We went back to her place after a while and fucked again, then she said her parents were going to be home soon. Let's go somewhere. No, I have to get ready for work. Kiss me here. Kiss me here. Ha-ha.

"What are you going to do?"

"Do?"

"Yeah, later. Not tonight but what are you doing working at a bar?"

"Oh, that's just for the summer. I'll go back to school in the fall."

I stood there.

"You can come see me at the bar tonight," she said.

I know, don't ask. Just stop it. Don't be a dick.

"Ah, I don't think so."

"Yeah, I know. The bands there suck. It was a hot place for a couple of years but the scene died out, went downtown. That's how it goes."

Call. I'll call. You better.

Kiss me here.

The concierge gave me a condescending look as I walked out. The street smelled good; I liked the street smell better than the library smell.

26

I tried it. I tried: You know uptown and downtown people and blend gracefully with all of them. You're on your way up, have purpose and promise. No, forget it. Let's go back downtown and forget it. No, don't hail a cab, walk. Let's look at all the people. New York is cool, look at the buildings. Someday Amy would be on TV, saying, "I knew a great man but lost him," and she'd sigh. No she wouldn't. Just forget it.

I hailed a cab and told him to drive downtown. Where? Anywhere, just head downtown. Where? All right, the West Village. Let's start there. Yeah, I'm a tourist. Just drive and I'll tell you. Got a cigarette?

"Yeah," he said and handed me one through the opening in the cage.

He started talking, giving me the tour. "It's cool, man. I like doing this. Nobody knows New York like a cabbie." He went on, "Most people hate it when I smoke, I like to smoke and talk. It gets boring, you know, you got money, right? We can drive all night and I'll show you around, man. It's cool."

He went on. No what do you do or anything, just mememe. I know this and that, it's my town.

We got stuck in traffic at 34th St. There was $3.60 on the meter and I handed him a five, got out.

"Herald Square," he said out the window.

I slipped quickly into the crowd and walked around aimlessly for hours. It felt good, being anonymous and ghost-like; I felt like a camera. You could be anything, nobody knows you, you could transform into somebody else. You could get some Chinatown huckster to make up several false ID's in his basement; driver's licenses, passports, birth certificates. The cage of life was too tight. People used to be able to just change their names and erase their histories and go into the frontier. But, there was no new frontier. Let's just walk around for a while and forget the leash. Look. All right. No, look.

*****

At twilight, I was in some Irish bar in the Chelsea district. The people there played darts and I thought of Nico and the Chelsea girls. They liked me, I could tell. Yeah, name's Diggs. Here's Flannigan and Boyle. There's some sad Irish tunes on the jukebox and some happy ones too. Play the sad ones.

"You know the luck of the Irish?"

"Yeah, bad luck."

Ah, yes, laddie. We'll play the sad ones then. That's how it goes. You stay awhile and drink with us and we'll listen to the sad ones. Don't go. I'll be right back, need some smokes. We have smokes.

"I'll be back," I said and went out.

Seventh Ave. was a river of southbound cars. Twilight playing on them, the sky, buildings. Hudson over there; a few blocks. The icecaps melted and we all swam. I.

Went for a walk, up the block, to the corner store, got cigs. We all swam. Gargoyles swooped. It's always like that at twilight. The sky changes color and the skin peels.

Off, let's go.

Listen to the fiddlers. They'll be there soon. Drink with the guests of the death ships.

All right, let's go. All right.

27 Get up off the floor. Yes, do that and then look out the window. It's raining; raining like all hell. Go take a piss, then go down to the bodega for coffee. The phone is ringing. Somebody should wake up and get the phone. Not me, it ain't my job.

When I got back with my coffee, Nick was sitting there at the desk and Choo was in the bathroom. They slept on bunk beds in the office that was supposed to be the living room. There was a kitchen but nobody ate there. There was a shower stall in the kitchen and a closet-sized bathroom next to the shower. Don slept in the back; the only room with a real door. I imagined the apartments in the building filled entire floors years ago before they were cut up into these little units. The whole East Village was like this, four to six story walk-ups, some got the original bathrooms and some got what they had there. Looks like they got the original kitchen here though.

Nick didn't say anything, was just sitting there. I didn't say anything, took my coffee and looked out the back window again. Three floors up with steel gates over it. In case of fire, unlock steel gate and run down fire escape. You could see the Trade Towers in the distance. You could see those fuckers driving in from Jersey a half hour before the tunnel.

"Where's the key?" I asked.

"What?" Nick said.

"The key to the gate."

"Oh hell, I dunno."

I sat down. Nick was rolling a joint. Choo-Choo came out of the bathroom and got into the shower.

We smoked the thing silently. After spending hours in the Irish bar the night before, I walked down to St. Mark's and found them at St. Mark's Bar & Grill. Then we closed the International at 4 am.

"I gotta go get something to drink," he said. "You want anything?"

"Beer."

"All right," he said and left.

We had talked about the band: you need to get up here where it's all happening, Nick said. You got a job when you do, Choo said. I dunno, I like the dollhouse, got it easy. Fuck that. But I got it easy for a while, okay, I know, you're right, just have to tidy up some things. All right, man! All right, Tony! Let's drink! Fuckin' hell, man. Drinkdrinkdrink...

I saw how it was and how it was gonna be. I'd do it anyway, what else was there? But it's no good being an outlaw, living in bars like they did. It's no damn good, a man needs something better. You need a chance; a fighting chance. If the only real chance you got is tenements, street life and bar life, you take it. What you gonna do anyway? Get married and settle down? Uh-huh, like you thought you were gonna do with Wendy. That was all right for a few years though; it was really love and caring for each other. It somehow didn't fit in with being a musician though, did it? No, they get jealous when they find out you love what you do better than them. You're gone all day at some job and then, the band is another job and then, you're home after another twelve hour day and they're missing the attention and getting mean and you try and say I'm doing this for us honey and she doesn't understand, feels slighted, like she's playing second fiddle to your dreams, you're a dreamer, she starts screaming at you and you're tired and lonely and a fuckhead anyway and all of a sudden, she's dragging you down. She might cook, clean and take care of everything else but she's dragging you down, you're dragging each other down, it's too much, without a dream you're dead, without me you're dead. We're dead. Uh-huh. Fuck.

There's Choo, getting out of the shower. Don't look. Oh, man, that guy's got a big dick. Don't look at it swinging under his scrawny, fifty-something frame. Don't hate him for it, even if he is queer. That fucker is funny, useta be a real hardcore drunk, so he said. Now he doesn't drink all day, just all night. Wrap a towel around yourself. Okay, after you dry your hair. That smells nice, what's that?

"It's a special shampoo I get from my hairdresser," he said.

Fucker lives in a dump and has a hairdresser. Makes big bucks running We Deliver, who knows how much? I can't think that far. Probably a lot. Rich and living in a dump. Don't know any better or doesn't care. Punk-ass probably doesn't care. Here comes Nick. He's got a six-pack and a couple cans of iced tea. He probably doesn't think about the shit I was just thinking about. I'm probably just some depressed navel-gazer, lost, so lost. Let's go somewhere and do something. Let's take our gear and set up in Madison Square Garden, it'll be nutty, fun. We can play for hours, days and we could get all your queer-assed buddies and messengers armed with machine guns to fight off the authorities. The TV news would show up and we wouldn't kill them, no. They'd put us on the airwaves and we'd keep playing. Our fingers would start bleeding and we wouldn't care and we'd eat mushrooms by the handful and the cops would lob tear gas and we'd laugh at them through a huge PA system which actually shook the building and women would bring us beer and food, they'd blow us and feed us while we kept playing through it all - we'd play 'til we died or got famous, then we'd sit in fine hotels in Europe (because we were de-ported) and drink girly drinks with our pinkies extended saying clever things that got printed in newspapers and magazines around the world.

"Want a beer?" Nick asked.

"Sure."

Don came out of the bedroom, said hi, grabbed his pack and bike from the kitchen, and left. It was his day on. The phones were ringing; Choo-Choo was on the phones. Don's girlfriend Jane came out of the bedroom and went into the bathroom, then disrobed and got in the shower. Nick looked at me. Yeah, so what?

"We could fuck her," Nick said.

"That's not right."

"No, we could. She's hot. Just watch her getting out of the shower."

"I've got to get back to PA today," I said.

"I thought you were staying for a few days?"

"Nah, I gotta get back. You wanna come down? I can call Lonnie, we can play, work on stuff."

"Fuck that. You guys need to get up here."

"I know that. We're here but all our stuff is down there and Lonnie's down there."

"I'll come down next weekend, like we planned. Man, I hate going down there. You know that, right?"

"I know," I said.

We sat there. Choo was talking on the phone.

"I don't hate it, but I don't want to come down this weekend."

We looked at Jane's shadow in the shower. Nick finished his tea and opened a beer.

"What's going on with Amy?" he asked.

"Nothing. We spent an afternoon together, I told you."

"You should…"

"Stop, it's no good. She's fine and nice but she's a rich girl. There's no way, I told you. Fuck it."

"All right, man! I know, it sucks. That's the way it is. Ha-ha! Man, you really like that girl, don't you?"

"Yeah, I really like her," I said. I wanted a cig but smoked a pack the night before. I didn't want a cig.

Jane got out of the shower and spent a while drying her hair. She looked over her shoulder and said, "Hi guys," then toweled off her chest. Then she bent over and toweled off her legs, putting one, then the other on the chair at the kitchen table nobody ever sat at. We all watched her, even Choo. Then she giggled a bit and went back to her room.

"I'm going back there to fuck her," Nick said.

"Goddamnit, Nicholas," Choo said.

"But Choo…"

"No."

"Oh, all right."

I picked up the phone and dialed Amy.

"Hello?" someone said.

"Hello, could I speak to Amy?"

"Who's this?"

"Tony."

I heard him yell for her. She picked up the phone.

"Hi, it's Tony."

"Oh, hi. What are you doing?"

They were sitting there, listening. I didn't like it.

"Nothing, I'm downtown. It's raining."

"Where are you?"

"At a friend's place. I was gonna head back to PA but wanted to call."

There was silence. "Can't you guys go someplace?" I said.

"It's my place," Choo said.

"What was that?" Amy asked.

"Nothing, was talking to my friends."

"Do you have to go back?"

"There's some trouble down there. I told another friend I would go back and take care of it."

There was more silence.

"We just met."

"You're going away to college and I'll never be a part of that world, your world. There's no way."

"There's ways."

"You think?"

"Yes, I think. I like you, I was thinking about you

and I'm glad you called."

"It's raining," I said.

"I know. I'm looking out the window."

She knew, was looking out the window too.

"Tony?"

"Yes?"

"My parents are going to the Hamptons for the weekend. They'll be leaving shortly."

"I'll be up," I said.

"Yes," she said and then was silent. We listened to each other breathing for a bit.

"Tony?" she finally whispered. "Hang up."

I put the phone in its cradle and sighed.

Nick and Choo were sitting there, smiling. "I'll never be a part of that world, your world, Nicholas," Choo said and then they both burst into laughter.

See? You're funny. Funnier'n hell. Aw, cut it out guys. Oh, god, we'll never be together. Ha-ha. Ha-haha. You fucks. Ha-ha. Goddamnit, Tony! All right, already.

The phones started ringing again. I grabbed my shit and made for the door.

"If ya get tired of playing with your uptown woman, come on down to the Int tonight," Choo said between phones.

"Yeah, Tony," Nick said. "I thought you were gonna hang with us anyway. Don't leave us like this, be a part of our world!"

Look at this dick walking in the rain. What the hell's wrong with him? Hey, blondie. Hey. Get yourself an umbrella, blondie! Ha-ha! Yeah, at least get a hat! I didn't see you looking at our women, did I? Yeah, but just their butts. Ha-ha, you okay blondie. This dickhead's got friends in the underworld and uptown women in two states. He'll always be a houseboy, a gigolo, he don't know any better. Now he's walking in the rain, thinking he'll get a cab up on 1st Ave. When it rains, all the cabs get taken, house-boy. Why don't you fantasize some cab? You're good at that kinda shit. Yeah, go on.

I stood there in the rain, getting wetter and wetter trying to hail cabs. The traffic rolled by and every once in a while, I'd be next to some puddle and get hit by the spray. I kept walking up 1st Ave and trying to get a cab. It seemed that some, most, knew the game. They'd stand there under their umbrellas in some fine clothes and the cabs would dive at them, like fish food. They'd cross three lanes in dangerous traffic to get at them. I watched the cabs dive and swoop like that, always passing me by, and I'd look at the people that got into them. They were some-how untouched by the rain and their surroundings, had some grace, some kind of class I didn't have. I didn't hate them for it, just made a mental note and walked down into the 14th St. subway station, soaking wet.

"I want to go to the Upper West Side," I told the man at the booth and handed him a dollar.

He gave me a token and a quarter back and said, "Next."

Someone started pushing at my back. "He said 'Next,'" the twerp said.

I ignored him and again asked the guy in the booth which train to take uptown, to the West Side. He gave me some glassy-eyed look, like I had almost woken him up.

"Just get on the train," he said.

"But..."

"I'll call a cop," he said. "I have a buzzer."

"Get out of the way," the twerp behind me again said and pushed at my back.

I turned around and told the twerp to wait, I wasn't done and the guy in the booth reiterated, "Don't start no trouble, I'll call a cop, I mean it."

I walked away, put my token in the turnstile and went

through. There were some people there waiting, and I asked some. They just looked at me funny, like I was insane, so I stood there and wrung out my hair, shook my clothes off like a dog. The trains came and went. I didn't know where they went or what I was doing. Finally, some girl walked up and stood next to me. "Hi," she said.

I was almost dry by this point, had been standing there like an idiot for a while.

"Hi," I said.

"You been waiting long?"

I told her I was lost, didn't know what the fuck and she told me the trains to take uptown. That I had to take this one west and then take that one from Union Square but don't get on the express and this and that. It was really complicated. I pretended to listen and understand and she said, "This is my train," and went off to Brooklyn. I wasn't even in the right station; I had to leave, cross the street and go down into the westbound station; had to get another token.

I walked down from 96th St. It was quite a while later. This time, I stayed away from the puddles and car splash. There's the concierge. "Hi."

Name please? You don't remember me? Name please? Adams. And you are? Tony, Tony Diggs. Yes sir, go on up. I'll just walk around in the courtyard in the rain. No, go on. Hello, Jimmy. Jimmy don't say nothing, what's with Jimmy?

Amy: "It's okay, Jimmy."

Jimmy nods, takes his sleigh back down the elevator shaft. Bye Jimmy.

Amy: "We're going to have to get you cleaned up."

Right. Let's go. Shower and lunch, we'll spend the weekend in bed. We'll send Jimmy for wine. You no got wine? My parents don't keep alcohol in the house. AA. Driver's club? No, silly. AA. Their faces like crisp bacon. That's not right. Look at me.

"Food too, I'm starving."

"We'll send Jimmy for food. You got any weed?"

"No, I'm all out."

"I want some weed."

"Got any money?"

"I have money."

"I'll make a call," I told her and got Choo on the line and he said half an hour.

Half hour. We'll wait. You know people? Yeah. Let's get your clothes in the wash and you in the shower. All right. Jimmy'll get the wine, food and your clothes, what do you want? Anything. Chinese? Whatever, I got nothing. That's all right, you just get in the shower. You too. No, look at me, get in the shower. Kiss me here. Kiss me here. Ha-ha, you're getting me all wet. We'll spend the weekend in bed.

Look at me.

28

The Broadway Limited was one of the last remnants from the old days when rail travel had style. It ran from NYC to Chicago, didn't stop at many of the stops the other trains did, and you didn't have to switch trains at 30th St. Station in Philadelphia. There was history on that train that I could feel in my bones. I had heard tales of my grandfather on my mother's side working for the railroad, and tales of my great-grandfather on my father's side working the rails after the Civil War, that he had been there, with a gang of displaced Irish, when they drove the golden spike to make the transcontinental railroad.

You just go on now, just ride the train and feel it. There's John L. Sullivan in the bar car with Diamond Jim Brady. They got pinky rings and fine suits, eh? My great-grandpa got his arm blown off in the Civil Car. Yeah, that's what I heard. Fucker drank like all hell too and swung the sledge one-handed. Mighta changed names after the Irish troubles, who knows? Yeah, the gene pool got watered down a bit. They had fight but got beaten down. I didn't know them, they're all dead; what I know is too sad, let's just forget it. Let's ride the train.

I had another beer in the bar car and looked at the shit in my wallet. Amy's phone number at home and at college. Her address at college, Stanford, somewhere in California. You don't know where Stanford is? No. Haha, you dolt. Look at me. We spent the weekend in bed. Jimmy brought us wine and food. That's not right. Oh, Jimmy likes doing things for me. That's not right. Haha, he likes it.

I spent a lot of time looking at the ceiling. There were the books in the library and we visited Charles Henri Ford again, who decided he liked me for some damn reason after I went off on a long monologue about this and that, the band, writing, oh, yes, I read this and that, I used to read a lot. A lot? Yeah, a whole fuckin' lot, whole libraries. School? Fuck them. Ha! Yes. Fuck them! He went off about this and that, he had really lived, had marvelous tales of the famous and fabulous. It was too much, I was outclassed. Tea. Yes, tea. Wine? No. All right. Tea.

"I must show you some things," he said.

Hours. Amy breathing. We went back and fucked and then I had to wait, build it back up again. She smoked dope. I didn't feel like it. "I quit," I told her. She shrugged and smoked by herself. Eat and fuck and wine. Let's go. Show me around. Show yourself around. I like you. You can't say it, can you? No, you're going away. You're going away. Look at me. This is wonderful.

The ceiling.

Let's just throw her number away. Yeah, do that. Forget it.

"You got a trash can?" I asked the bartender.

"Yeah, there," he pointed.

I wadded the paper with her numbers and addresses up into a ball. Then I smoothed it out on the bar and looked at it again. Then I put it back in my wallet.

The ride through New Jersey was smooth and fast. There were people in the bar car with me and conversation. After a few beers I told marvelous lies that I soon forgot. It didn't matter; strangers on a train. Many got off in Philadelphia and I went back to my seat. Some other people got on; I didn't want to talk, was done talking.

The ride back to Harrisburg was bumpier and slower. I called Cindy when I got there.

"Tony! Where have you been? I thought you were coming back Saturday!"

"I told you I might stay for a while."

"No you didn't."

"I didn't?"

"No."

"Well, look. Can you come get me?"

"You're at the train station?"

"Yes. Please come get me."

She said she would and hung up. She sounded frantic. I walked outside and waited. A while later, she pulled up in her mom's car and told me I should drive. I threw my pack in the back and drove.

"You're wired," I said.

"Oh fuck, Tony. Dwayne's taken over my house."

"You're wired, you look wired. That cocaine will make you crazy, girl!"

"You weren't there! I didn't know what to do!"

"Did Tim come with the money on Friday? I'm broke."

"He gave it to me and I spent it."

"Coke?"

"Goddamnit, Tony! You weren't there."

I looked at her. "I'll take care of it, don't worry."

"You aren't mad?"

"No, I'm not mad. I know how it is."

I drove across the river and past her place.

"Where are you taking me?

"Let's go down by the river for a bit," I said.

"We have to get back. It's crazy there!" she said.

"No, we have to go where I drive," I said and drove down by the river, past where we went swimming a while back. There was a parking lot under the Rockville Bridge. People would park there and launch boats from the shore. I parked and told her to get out. She did and I came around to her side and took her hand.

"Let's go for a walk," I said.

"Goddamnit, Tony."

"No, forget it. Just forget it for a bit."

We walked to the river's edge and I found some loose stones, skipped them into the water.

"You talk to your mom yesterday?"

"Yes. She called."

"How is she?"

"Oh hell, I don't know. She says she's better but decided to stay two more months; that she's not ready to leave yet, needs the people there. Her support group. Such shit."

"No way. I thought she was coming back next week."

"Nope. She asked about you, if you were holding up your end of the deal."

"Am I?"

"Yeah, you have been. That's what I told her. She said she was sorry she missed you and hoped you would be in next Sunday when she called."

I looked at her arms. "Heroin too?"

"Oh fuck, Tony. We got some good shit at the house. You want to... Oh, never mind. You probably don't."

"No, I do. That's the trouble. You do that and nothing else matters. I been there. We both have."

"We were doing so good," she said.

"Just forget it. You remember that night we danced? When you were still getting over the operation?"

"Yeah. That was nice."

It was late afternoon and the shadows of the trees were falling off our backs and into the river. There were birds flying about and some egrets out there.

"I really like it here," I said.

"I like being here with you," she said, and then added: "I'm sorry; I went crazy."

"We all went crazy, whatever that is. Fuck it. The world is crazy and we're in the world."

We walked along and I skipped more stones into the river. "Five. I did a five-skip. You see that?"

"You're a real sportsman."

"So now you know."

"Tony?"

"What?"

"Could you hold me?" she asked, and stood there looking frightened, shattered. Like I would tell her no.

I held her and we stood there by the water's edge for the longest time like that, trying to drag the good parts out of each other. A small boat pulled up and two fishermen got out and looked at us. The one guy said something ignorant and the other guy said, "Leave 'em alone, Bob," and smiled at us. Cindy and I unlocked and watched them drag their boat up onto a trailer.

"You get anything?" I asked.

"Channel cats. Bigguns," the one guy said. "Wanna see?"

We went to take a look. They had some big-ass catfish in a pail.

We talked for a bit and then they drove off.

"Who's over at your house?" I asked Cindy.

"Dwayne and some Philadelphia guy. They set up shop there. I wanted to get rid of them but was lonely and they gave me some free drugs. Then the fuckers started charging me and they got this other guy, a dope dealer over. They pretty much took over and no matter what I say, they won't leave."

"What happened to your girlfriend? What's her name, Toni?"

"She took off, couldn't deal with it. Hell, she was just a lesbo anyway, not a druggie."

"She was cute."

"She hated you and men in general. Damnit Tony, these guys are packed."

"Packed?"

"They got guns, man. They got people coming day and night to score and they let them stay. I got junkies and coke fiends laying around my house, shooting dope, smoking coke. It's really fucked up."

"Cindy?"

"Yes?"

"Let's go clean house," I said.

29

Dwayne was there to greet us when we got back.

"Hey, Tony! How was the gig in New York City?" he asked like an old friend.

"It was all right. What's going on here, Dwayne?"

"Oh, nothing much, just taking care of business. Cindy's been good enough to give us a base of operation for a while. Right, Cindy?"

"Whatever, Dwayne," she said and hung on my arm.

"Who are all these people?" I asked Dwayne.

"This is Stephen, he's from Philadelphia, and this is Duke, he's from Pittsburgh. Say hello to my friend Tony, guys."

They said hi and stood there.

"Who are all these other people?" I asked.

"They're customers," Stephen said.

"I wasn't talking to you," I said. "I was talking to Dwayne."

"They're customers, Tony," Dwayne said. "Don't disrespect my friends."

"I remember you when you were a snot-nosed kid following us around the suburbs," I said to Dwayne.

He scratched his nose, gave a little heh-heh, and said, "You had to go there, didn't you? It ain't like that anymore. You don't know, man."

"Cindy, go to your room," I said.

She kissed me on the cheek and went up the stairs. I walked around the living room a bit and people said hey. They all looked stoned. There were needles and pipes lying about.

"All you people have to leave now," I said.

They looked at me like who the hell are you?

"Ya'll gotta go," I said to Dwayne and them.

"Tony, Tony. We ain't going nowhere," Dwayne said. "Just cut it out. I know you like the dope; we got dope, man, it's cool. We'll turn you on for free. Right, guys?"

Stephen and Duke just looked at me. Duke said, "I could throw you a bag or so."

"Whatcha gonna do? Try and kick our asses?" Stephen said. Dwayne and Duke busted out in laughter. Several of the customers laughed also.

Stephen pulled a gun out of his belt and pointed it at me, saying what a funny motherfucker I was. I grabbed his hand, shoved it toward the ceiling and punched him in the throat. The gun came out in my hand cleanly and he fell to the floor. Duke was pulling his piece out of his belt; I blew a cap in his leg, jumped over the coffee table, grabbed him by the throat and put Stephen's gun to his head. He pointed his gun at the floor and I took it from his hand. There was a lot of yelling and moaning. The customers started grabbing up their paraphernalia.

"EVERYBODY JUST FREEZE!" I yelled.

They did. I stood there with a gun in each hand and backed toward the wall.

"Shit, Tony!" Dwayne said.

"SHUT UP!"

It got real quiet except for Stephen choking on the floor. Duke had his hands on his leg. They were bloody and his jeans were getting wet with piss.

"You guys on the couch can leave," I said.

They gathered their shit and left quickly.

"Are there any other people in the house? Anyone upstairs?" I asked Dwayne.

"No."

"I'll cap you if you're lying."

"You ain't gonna shoot me, man. We're friends."

"Were friends. You bring this garbage in the house I live in and try and fuck with me? I told you fuckers to leave but no, you gotta be tough guys."

"I'll kill you," Duke said.

"Shut up and give me your money and dope, all of it.

Put it on the coffee table. Get Stephen's too."

"You're gonna pay for this," Duke said.

I walked over and shot him in the foot of his bad leg. He screamed.

"I'd shoot you again but you're bleeding enough. Just shut up and do as I say."

They started piling money and drugs on the table. Dwayne dug into Stephen's pockets and got his. Stephen was having a hard time breathing; it looked like he wouldn't make it.

"CINDY!" I yelled. I heard her door open and she poked her head downstairs.

"Is everything all right?" she asked.

"Check all the upstairs rooms. If there's anyone up there, yell. I'll come up and shoot them."

"Okay, Tony!" she said.

"That's all of it, Tony," Dwayne said, placing the last of the stuff on the table.

I told them to stand against the wall and wait while I had a seat and looked at it. There was what looked like a couple thousand dollars as well as a half ounce of cocaine and twenty-some bags of heroin.

"All clear up here!" Cindy yelled. "Should I come down now?"

"No, wait!" I yelled back upstairs.

"I'll go to my room," she said.

I heard the door shut.

"All right, you guys can go now. Take your friend. I don't need anyone dying here."

They helped him out. Dwayne said, "You ain't heard the last of this," as he was leaving.

"Yeah," Duke said.

"Uh-huh," I said and watched them get Stephen in his car. After they all drove off, I stood there watching for a while yet to see if they might loop around, come back. They didn't.

"You can come out now!" I yelled upstairs.

Cindy poked her head downstairs and said, "Is the house clean?"

"Yeah, mostly. Come on down."

She bounded down the stairs. "I heard gunfire."

"That was me," I said.

"Tony? You think you could put them down now?"

"I didn't realize," I said and put the guns on the table.

"That's okay, honey. You shoot somebody?"

"Yeah, fuck. Had to."

We sat on the couch and I told her what happened while I counted the money.

"Got a cigarette?"

"I don't smoke," she said.

"That's right. Here," I said and handed her $1200.

"What's this?"

"Half. I wasn't planning on robbing them; was just gonna kick them out. But then they had to piss me off. I woulda killed 'em all if I weren't so lazy."

"Yeah. Lugging dead bodies around is a real hassle."

"What? I was just thinking about how we were gonna explain it to the cops."

"Oh, right. Yeah, I guess we would have had to call the cops, he-he."

"Ha-ha."

"Well?" she said, looking at all the drugs on the table.

"Shit," I said.

"Yeah, I know. We better just flush it."

"Let's keep a few bags of smack," I said. "Just maybe..."

"Tony?"

"Shit."

"All right. We keep a few and some cokes."

"No coke."

"Damnit, Tony. I like it."

"Let's not argue."

"All right. The hell with it," she said.

We ended up keeping ten bags of smack and ten quarter-grams of coke. We flushed the rest. I gave her the .32 after checking it and telling her about the safety. I kept the 9mm with the fourteen round clip, twelve rounds left. There was no food in the house; what was there had gone bad. She started cleaning up and throwing things away and I said I'd go get food.

So there it is. You're driving down the road in your girl-friend's mother's BMW with $1200 and change in your pockets. Her mother is your girlfriend also. And then there's that rich girl in Manhattan. All you need is one more to even it out. They can draw and quarter you when they're done and then go do lesbo stuff.

I took a left at Front St. and drove over to the super-market. It might take a while, a few weeks but, the guys you robbed will be back. They weren't kidding. Ah, hell – it'll take a while. They'll need doctors and healing and some time before the hang-up phone calls and then the drive-bys. You might have to attack them instead of waiting around. That would be the smart thing.

When I got back with the food, Cindy had the place pretty well cleaned up. I took out the trash bags and she started dinner. A chicken casserole thing, I had gotten everything she needed. We talked in the kitchen while it was cooking. I lit a cig and took a few drags, put it out.

"We could have kept all the drugs and sold them," she said.

"Uh-huh."

"He-he."

"Yup. Let's just take it easy tonight."

"Right; you're right."

"Cindy? Do you have any works in the house?"

"I threw them out," she said, "with the other shit."

"Good. You don't want a hit right now?"

"Yes, I want one so bad. I want to slam dope and snort coke 'til it's all gone but you're here. You ground me Tony. You hungry?"

"I'm freakin' starving."

"I'm gonna feed you. It'll be good, you'll see. And, Tony?"

"Yes?"

"Thanks for getting rid of those guys."

I picked up the cig and relit it. "It was nothing," I said.

She stood there looking at me, and then turned to make a salad. She stopped, looked back at me with a puzzled look on her face. Then she went back to making the salad. "You like ranch dressing?" she asked with her back to me.

"Sure. It's fine."

"You ever shoot anyone before?"

"No."

"What did it feel like?"

I took a drag off the cig.

"It felt ugly," I said. "I hated it."

She looked back at me and said, "Uh-huh."

The sun was rolling into the horizon when we ate at the picnic table out back. It spilled out all red before it dipped over the edge.

30

We never did do the Pot Parade gig. It didn't matter anyway; those Yippies were burnouts. And those guys never came back gunning for me like I thought they would. I ran into Dwayne on the street a few months later and he said that Stephen went back to Philadelphia and Duke went back to Pittsburgh. Dwayne wasn't pissed at me. He thanked me.

"I got my shit together after that night," he said, explaining how he was selling insurance now.

"Insurance?"

"Yeah, man. Some other people I dealt with got busted. It was time to get out."

He laughed and told me that that night, he didn't give me any of his money. "You just got theirs. Fuck them, they deserved it."

We agreed to meet a little later in some bar. He had some things to do and I was going to see someone about a place to stay. Fucking insurance.

I went and talked to the guy and he showed me the room in the rooming house where Sandman still lived. $65 a month. I paid him and moved in the next day with Lonnie's help.

I never did any of the drugs we saved; Cindy did them all then she was on the phone again looking when they ran out. Lois came home and fell right back into drinking like a fish. It was too much.

My new place was a half block from the river; the guy from upstairs' old room. He lost his job for stealing from the hospital and left town. I had the old couch from our practice room for a bed and found an old desk by some dumpster and got a phone, a chair. I had some money saved and had gotten my car fixed and inspected. It was just a small room but it was mine. The others in the rooming house were okay, old guys, drunks. Sandman had quit fucking with junk but still smoked weed and collected records and sold them. I didn't smoke pot anymore; had quit everything.

I started running by the river. It was a slow go at first; I was really out of shape but kept at it. I'd run and do pushups and situps. There was a diner a few blocks away where I'd go for lunch, read the paper, look at the want ads like I wanted a job. Brenda was the waitress and Sophie, who owned the place, was the cook. I always tipped Brenda well. One day, Sophie asked what I did.

"I'm a writer," I told her.

"We had you pegged for a musician."

That was the day I went to the drug store and bought some fresh notebooks and pens and went home, looked at the empty pages. I'd told Cindy I'd assassinate her and told Sal I wanted to be a writer. I was no damn writer, just a singer/songwriter and not too good at that. Nick came down on weekends to play up at Lonnie's. He started bringing down this sax player. Then, the sax player was in the band.

"I'll move soon."

"You have a job when you do," Nick said.

I never went to the dollhouse again. I called Amy in California once, then Amy called all the time from California, saying I should move out there to be with her. Weeks went by with her calling me nightly and us talking for hours, then the calls stopped. I started going to the bar around the corner nightly. There were people and madness and the notebooks started filling up with things but it wasn't right, I wasn't getting it. Time and money were running out.

Then Amy was on the phone again. Well?

"Well what?"

"You know."

"Give me your address."

She told me and I wrote it down. She said she didn't live in the dorm, had a nice apartment and I found myself saying I'd be driving out there the next day. Palo Alto.

"Below San Francisco. You have a map?"

"Yeah."

"Oh honey, this is going to be wonderful! I'm so happy!"

It was late that night, after packing and deciding to leave everything there except my clothes and notebooks. I was walking home from the bar and heard, "TONYYY!" from a car that was driving by with music blaring. She waved from the passenger window.

"CINDYYY!" I yelled.

"TONYYYYY!" she yelled again. "WOO-HOOO!"

"WOO-HOOO!" I yelled at her and into the endless night.

Printed in the United States
95415LV00002B/19/A